Praise for Maria Grace

"Grace has quickly become one of my favorite authors of Austen-inspired fiction. Her love of Austen's characters and the Regency era shine through in all of her novels." *Diary of an Eccentric*

"Maria Grace is stunning and emotional, and readers will be blown away by the uniqueness of her plot and characterization." *Savvy Wit and Verse*

"Maria Grace has once again brought to her readers a delightful, entertaining and sweetly romantic story while using Austen's characters as a launching point for the tale." *Calico Critic*

"I believe that this is what Maria Grace does best, blend old and new together to create a story that has the framework of Austen and her characters, but contains enough new and exciting content to keep me turning the pages. ... Grace's style is not to be missed." *From the desk of Kimberly Denny-Ryder*

Inspiration

Maria Grace

White Soup Press

Published by: White Soup Press

Inspiration
Copyright © 2019 Maria Grace

For information, address
author.MariaGrace@gmail.com

ISBN-13: 978-0692530955 (White Soup Press)

Author's Website: RandomBitsofFaascination.com
Email address: Author.MariaGrace@gmail.com

Dedication

For my husband and sons.
You have always believed in me.

Chapter 1

DARCY SET DOWN his paintbrush and flexed his shoulders, his cravat constricting his throat as he did. The comforting, lingering, nutty scent of linseed oil hung in the air at the edges of his awareness, almost unnoticeable after hours of smelling it. How long had he been staring at the rough sketch on his canvas? Judging by the shadows the two easels cast on the scuffed wood floor and the vague chill that had crept into the air, it had been hours.

The light through the attic windows was waning. Might as well stop the exercise in futility now.

"Are you finished?" Charles Bingley peeked around his easel and waved a paintbrush at Darcy, flinging little gobbets of ocher paint onto the floor. Was that how he had managed to get paint in his hair as well?

That sort of mess was precisely why he did not

bother to have this floor properly finished, and the room was largely devoid of furnishings except the easels, stools, and what was used to store his supplies.

"Hardly." Darcy turned his back and fiddled with his paints. Ultimately a servant would come and clean up for him, but perhaps if he appeared occupied, Bingley would not continue to press for conversation.

"I cannot thank you enough for inviting me to use your studio space. You were right. The attics at Darcy House offer the most marvelous light in the whole of London, I should say." Bingley wiped his hands on his paint-stained apron and sauntered toward him. Even his confident steps sounded intrusive.

Darcy grumbled and muttered under his breath.

"Still blocked, are you?" Bingley inspected Darcy's work from several angles. "Not a lick of paint on the canvas all morning?"

"As you can see." No, it was not polite to snarl, but Bingley had earned it.

Bingley pulled Darcy's high stool close and perched one hip on it. "I am hardly the artist you are, but even I can see you are in quite a muddle here. You have never been so hindered in all the time I have known you. Back at university, you were at the easel every spare moment you had, producing quite accomplished works regularly. You could have made quite a living as a painter had you not already been a gentleman."

"How kind of you to remind me of the height from which I have fallen." Darcy rolled his eyes and turned his back on Bingley.

"I am worried about you. Never have I seen anything drive you to distraction as this seems to have."

"Should I thank you for stating the obvious?"

Darcy dropped his brush. A large smear of burnt umber appeared on the floor where it fell.

"Let me help you."

He whirled to face Bingley. "And exactly how do you propose to do that? Will you take my hand in yours and apply paint to the canvas for me?"

Bingley laughed, that easy, warm chuckle he had always had. His good nature could be maddening at times like these. "Hardly. It is no secret that I will never be the sort of artist you are—and that I do not resent you for your talent, which is quite big of me, I would say. I dabble for my own amusement, but you—you paint as though your very life and soul were poured into the efforts, as though it were a matter of life and breath that you create your works. And it is tearing you to pieces that you have produced nothing in—how long is it now?"

"Six months." The words sounded like a death sentence.

"So then, allow me to help you."

"What do you propose?" Why did he even ask? There was nothing anyone could do until this awful bleakness passed of its own accord.

"You have been ensconced in this studio for months with nothing but the confines of London to inspire you. You need to get away. The countryside is always inspiring. Come with me to Hertfordshire. I mean to rent a house there, get the feel of having an estate, you know. I could use your advice. And if Netherfield Park is suitable, you can stay with me there. Perhaps the change in venue will present you with some heretofore elusive inspiration."

The idea was dreadful and intriguing all at the same time. Leaving London meant travel, and that was inconvenient. And it meant dealing with people, meeting with them, interacting with them, probably hating them. All of which were also inconvenient and uncomfortable.

But staying in town was doing him no good, either. "I suppose I can accompany you before I return to Pemberley."

The journey to Hertfordshire had not been unpleasant—a few hours on horseback in fine September weather were good for the soul. And what was good for the soul was also good for one's muse. Certainly, it—she—had not been resurrected, not yet, but there were vague stirrings within, the kind related to creative energies, not the revenge of last night's supper.

Perhaps Bingley was right. There was something about the countryside, or perhaps it was being in an unfamiliar place with so much potential for discovery. Whatever it was, artistic surges bubbled and teased, tickled and prodded his heart and mind as they had not in months. For that reason alone, he would have recommended that Bingley take Netherfield, no matter how dreadful the establishment.

Luckily, the house and grounds were good, so he could make his endorsements with a clear conscience.

After just over a fortnight in the country, it was difficult to pronounce Bingley right or wrong. Darcy had produced two landscapes—one of the Netherfield house itself—and a still life of some random bric-a-brac scavenged from various rooms of the house. They were journeyman's efforts at best, hardly anything to be proud of and certainly not satisfying to behold. But they were the first completed works he had produced since Easter and the dreaded visit to Rosings Park.

It was difficult not to curse Aunt Catherine for that.

Perhaps that was the source of his troubles now. Ever since she started pushing him to fix a date for his wedding to Anne, all creative compulsions had ceased. But how could they not? Contemplating life fixed to that dry, wizened shell of a woman who scarcely had an original idea. By Jove, she barely said a word of her own volition! His soul withered in his chest every time he shared space with her. How could he possibly be expected to live like that?

Chest tightening, aching at the very thought, he paced his spacious guest quarters. Perhaps he could outrun the sensation before he resorted to canceling his plans.

Bingley pounded on his door. "Are you nearly ready, Darce? The ladies are in the parlor waiting for us."

Darcy glanced in the mirror and straightened his cravat, the sense of suffocation fading. His valet had done a good job tonight. Not that he had anyone to impress in this quaint market town, but being properly attired was a comfort of its own. "I am coming directly."

Bingley's distinct footfalls strode away.

A simple country assembly should not be such a trial; surely, none would agree it was something to be dreaded. And yet it was so. Dancing with unfamiliar partners was abhorrent and, truth be told, embarrassing. Inevitably, he would find himself staring at his partner, analyzing the shape of her eyes, the lines of her nose, the usually imperfect symmetry of her face, considering how it might be subtly and skillfully improved when rendered in charcoal or crayon or paint.

Such attentions, when noticed, were bad enough, but heaven help him if his eyes drifted lower, to necklines that were far too intriguing in the ways they played with light and shadow. No young lady had ever been able to accept that such attentions were artistic, not—ah, more personal in nature. They expected he meant far more than he ever did, and it never ended well.

Perhaps tonight, though, with his muse not quite fully awakened, he could avoid such uncomfortable encounters. If not, there was always the card room.

Bingley's coach trundled along the carriage line on the approach to the assembly rooms. Ordinary and unassuming was the best that could be said of the building. Absolutely the best. The rest was not appropriate to dwell upon and could very well poison him for the rest of the evening.

After all, how was one to enjoy himself in an environment so drab, dreary, and awkward? Was not beauty an essential quality of any such event?

They picked their way across the muddy, rutted street and waited their turn to enter the assembly rooms. An uneven, tired blue covered the walls. It might have been as appealing as a robin's egg when newly painted, but now it just whimpered to leave it alone and let it rest. Scuffed, even gouged in places, the floors cried out for mercy. And the paintings littering the walls—enough! Such thoughts were absolutely not helpful.

Presently, a round-faced, red-cheeked, potbellied man wearing a Master of Ceremonies sash greeted them. He seemed a bit pompous, full of himself, as though he were at an assembly in Bath, offering to make introductions for them. Bingley readily agreed as Darcy stifled a sigh. But then, Bingley enjoyed meeting new people.

The whole experience of being paraded around and introduced was to be expected—and dreaded. It was simply what happened at such events. Still though, from the looks the party garnered—and the glances fixed on Darcy alone—it was clear that their servants had already taken care of circulating word of the general level of wealth and connections their party brought with them.

It should not bother him that the entire room seemed ready to approve of him and gladly admit him into their acquaintance on so little a recommendation. Aunt Catherine would have declared it was the right and proper reaction, and it was, in fact, their due for being part of the best society in England. Many would agree with her, but Darcy did not.

Beauty, in all its forms, and the admirable qualities that went with it, were often found quite outside such trivial circles. Many times, it lurked in unexpected arenas. But Aunt Catherine would hardly admit such uncouth ideas.

Now was definitely neither the time nor the place to chance discovering intriguing sorts of beauty. Acquainted with no one in the room, he could not risk it. So, he danced once with Mrs. Hurst, whose beauty was unremarkable to be sure, and once with Miss Bingley, who was attractive enough but in the ordinary sort of way of the upper class.

What would her reaction be if she knew he found her beauty common enough to be of little note? How angry she would be—then she might be of more interest. Women could be fascinating when they were angry—the subtle expressions of their eyes, the tension in their throats…but Miss Bingley would hardly appreciate such things.

Once he had danced those two sets, he spent the rest of the evening walking about the room, speaking only to those of his own party, much to the obvious disapproval of the denizens of Meryton. The way they looked at him and whispered among themselves! No doubt they had decided he was the proudest, most disagreeable man in the world.

It was not the first time he had seen those looks, and doubtless it would not be the last. At least at home in Derbyshire, he was better regarded, having had the opportunity to demonstrate his true character there. Perhaps, his muse willing of course, he would return there in a few weeks, able to pursue his art in the sanctuary of his own home surroundings.

He paused in his circuit around the room. Bingley had found a lovely partner, probably the prettiest girl in the room. He and she danced together particularly well. So well, in fact, that Bingley wore a decidedly puppyish smile as he gazed at her.

Lovely, he had found yet another "angel" for his attentions. What was her name? Miss Bennet? Whatever it was, they twirled their way in grace and elegance to the end of the line and paused, their turn to wait out a set of the music.

Bingley looked over his shoulder and sauntered toward Darcy. "Come, Darcy, I must have you dance. I hate to see you standing about by yourself in this stupid manner. You had much better dance."

Darcy pinched the bridge of his nose and turned aside. Why did Bingley have to make a public spectacle? "I certainly shall not. You know how I detest it, unless I am particularly acquainted with my partner. At such an assembly as this, it would be insupportable. Your sisters are engaged, and there is not another woman in the room whom it would not be a punishment for me to stand up with.'"

Bingley offered a sound that seemed half-chuckle, half-snort. "I would not be so fastidious as you are for a kingdom! Upon my honor, I never met with so many pleasant girls in my life as I have this evening; and there are several of them, you see, uncommonly pretty.'"

"You are dancing with the only handsome girl in the room." That was not entirely true. There were any number of handsome women, but all of them ordinary—the kind one might encounter anywhere. Entirely uninspiring.

"Oh! she is the most beautiful creature I ever beheld! But there is one of her sisters sitting down just behind you, who is very pretty, and I dare say very agreeable. Do let me ask my partner to introduce you."

"Which do you mean?" He looked over his shoulder.

Air rushed from his lungs, and his eyes lost focus. He blinked furiously. Heavens above! A nymph sat against the wall regarding the dancers. Her features favored Bingley's partner, but there was something different about her. Something remarkable. Something entirely unique that he had never seen before.

Something he had to paint. His fingers tingled, and his hands twitched.

She looked up at him and caught his eye. Blast and botheration! He had been caught staring. But her reaction was so peculiar. She did not blush or stammer or otherwise try to garner his notice or call attention to the fact he had been staring. She merely smiled with a tiny nod. What ever could she mean?

He looked away and spoke just a little louder. "She is tolerable; but not handsome enough to tempt *me*. I am in no humor at present to give consequence to young ladies who are slighted by other men. You had better return to your partner and enjoy her smiles, for you are wasting your time with me." Of course, he did not mean a word of that, but what else could he have possibly said when Bingley was ready to be far more helpful than Darcy could tolerate?

Bingley rolled his eyes and drew breath for what would surely be one of his lengthy diatribes, but the first notes of the next repetition of the music drew him back to his partner and delivered Darcy from an unpleasant conversation—at least for the moment.

The young woman had turned her shoulder toward him, probably thinking she was delivering some sort of subtle cut. But he could hardly have asked for more. From this angle, he could study the intriguing line of her neck and back, the graceful craft of her ear and the barest suggestion of the silhouette of her face. His heart beat a little faster. How much longer before he could be away from this place and back to his paints?

The next morning Darcy woke at dawn. The rest of the household would sleep until noon or even later after such a late night. But how could he sleep when his muse called? All night he had dreamt of laying brush to canvas; he could not wait a moment more. His heart would surely burst if he did.

He rushed through his morning toilette without his valet, who would only distract him and further complicate the muddle of his thoughts. He forced himself to think of each step lest he miss something significant as his mind struggled to leap ahead to the project he had completed in his dreams. If only he had brought his oils, but for now watercolor must do. Perhaps there was a decent colorman's shop in Meryton.

At last, his canvas perched on his easel in a beam of morning sun. Trembling fingers tightened around a pencil as he sucked in a deep breath. There was something almost sacred about a pristine canvas. The act of marking it could be almost profane, especially when inspiration eluded him. But now … now was different. The pencil glided down, around, over, through curves, with a hint of shadow. It seemed only moments later that the rough blocked forms of a nymph admiring her reflection in a reflecting pool took shape.

Yes! Yes, exactly as he had seen it in his mind's eye. His fingers tingled as power surged through eyes, arms, and hands, colors and images taking shape before him.

"Darcy? Darcy…"

Darcy jumped, nearly dropping his brush. "What

are you doing here? I understand I am in your house, but since when has that negated the need to knock on a closed door?"

"Since I have been knocking for a full five minutes with no answer from you." Bingley stood just behind him.

"You jest."

"Not at all. I would wager you have been at your easel since dawn by the look of you." Bingley's right eye twitched with something of a wink.

"What of it?"

"Have a look outside. What do you notice about the sun?"

Darcy blinked and peered out of the window. No, that was not possible. Surely only an hour, maybe two had passed.

"It is nearly sundown, and you have no idea. It has been quite some time since I have seen you this way." Bingley peered over Darcy's shoulder. "I can see why. Very impressive. I have never seen this sort of work from you—it is inspired, truly inspired. You almost expect the nymph to rise up off the painting daring you to give her chase. I only wish I could see her face."

"Her face?" Something crushed his chest, leaving him dizzy and weak.

"Yes, you have painted her from a distance, behind and to the side. Did you not even realize that?"

Darcy stared at the painting as if for the first time. Bingley was right, her face was hidden, just barely silhouetted against the trees. It was not meant to be seen, it was part of the mystery of the scene. But what if she turned? What would that be like?

"Wait, wait, I know that look in your eye. You are

already sketching the next work in this series. Do not deny it; I can tell. Before you get any farther in the process, I insist you come down to dinner. You have eaten nothing today, and knowing you, you will eat nothing if not forced until this inspiration is complete. So, consider yourself forced, and come down right now. The light is gone in any case. You can do no more today."

Darcy grumbled under his breath. But Bingley was right. There was not enough light for real work tonight. He might as well eat. He would bring his sketchbook down to the parlor, though—firelight was sufficient for that endeavor. That way he could make the time he would have to sit with his host and his sisters at least somewhat productive.

Nearly a month passed with Darcy scarcely leaving his guest chambers at Netherfield. Canvasses— finished, partially finished, and barely started—littered every available space. His sketchbook lay open on the floor, taunting him.

With each additional creative effort, his tensions mounted. The sort of tensions that were energetic and addictive, that kept drawing him back. Fitzwilliam had once seen him in such a state and likened him to an opium eater. There was probably more truth in the comparison than Darcy would have preferred.

At first, it had been a delightful tension of anticipation—a new work in progress, the thrill of the creative, generative act. The wonder at what it would become, what new secrets would he learn from the images that formed beneath his brush. But as the weeks passed, the sweetness slipped away, replaced by bitter frustration.

He stared at the canvas before him and growled, searching the room for what he needed, but naturally it was not there, hiding in the shadows of the late afternoon sun. Bingley had been right. Infuriatingly right. He clutched his paintbrush in a grip that drove the blood from his fingers and sank down on his stool to cover his face with his hand.

The nymph needed to show her face. The image, the story, was painfully incomplete without a glimpse of the expression she wore as she sat beside that infernal pond, thinking who knew what. He had to know—he simply had to.

Yet she refused to show her face. He scrubbed his face with his hands.

He had seen Miss Bennet's face, but his muse somehow hid it from him each time he looked for it in his memories. It was there; it had to be. But stubborn minx that she was, she refused to show it to him. He threw aside his brush, allowing it bounce off the drapery as it clattered to the floor. Nicolls, the housekeeper, would probably not appreciate the Prussian blue splotch on the curtains.

He rubbed his temples hard. What he needed was neither a meal, a glass of wine, or a bottle of brandy, nor perhaps all of them, as Bingley had suggested.

In truth, none of those would do anything but temporarily distract his misery. He needed to see Miss Elizabeth Bennet once again. Not just to see her, but to sit down and study her at length, to stare at her and memorize every feature, every expression, from the arch of her eyebrow to the line of her jaw, and everything in between. More than food or drink or possibly even air, everything in him required that he be permitted a prolonged audience with Miss Bennet.

One that could never, ever happen.

Bingley seemed to suspect his need, suggesting that they call upon Longbourn. His motive might have been a bit more self-serving than it seemed at first blush; he appeared quite smitten with the eldest Bennet sister. But even if he had gone along with Bingley's scheme, it would hardly have afforded him the opportunity he needed. And to be so close to his inspiration without being able to absorb her essence would be more than his tortured soul could tolerate.

So, he paced the floor and wrestled with images that would not cooperate. And cursed the day he allowed Bingley to convince him to take this ill-advised expedition. Then the rain came in, stealing his light and confining him to his room when Miss Bennet arrived to dine with Bingley's sisters. Yes, he could have joined them, but Miss Bennet looked just enough like her sister to ensure he would be driven mad. If he were not already there now, which was a distinct possibility.

Worse still, having been in the rain, the delicate maiden became ill and could not be moved from Netherfield. Perhaps he should simply jump from his window to end his suffering. That might be preferable to this anguish.

***

Finally, the rains stopped, and he could take a turn about the gardens. It was not likely to help, but very occasionally fresh air and natural beauty could assuage his tormented sensibilities, for at least a little while.

He buttoned his coat and pulled on his hat, hurrying down the stairs. Hopefully, he could make it out of the house without notice. Civil words—to anyone—were certainly beyond him.

Success! A dozen steps from the front door, he gulped in morning air tasting of old rain and open fields. He closed his eyes and breathed in the matching fragrance—green and loamy and earthy. Sheep in the distance bleated their greetings to one another, and a cow joined the conversation. Dogs barked to remind them all of their places. Home—this place had just the barest resemblance to home. There was something to be said about the countryside.

"Oh, excuse me!"

His eyes flew open. It could not be. But there she was, standing right in front of him, staring directly into his eyes! How? Why? What would make Providence smile upon him so?

"Mr. Darcy?" Her forehead knotted—a most intricate knot, one to be remembered.

He shook his head and blinked. "Yes, yes. Pray forgive me, I did not expect to see you there."

"I suppose not. I came to call upon my sister." She dipped in the barest of curtsies.

"Your sister? Oh, yes, your sister. I did not see her myself, but I heard she fell ill yesterday after the rains."

"I came to see for myself how she is doing and if perhaps she might be removed to Longbourn for her recovery."

No, she must not be removed, not for any reason, not if it brought Miss Elizabeth here! "I … yes … that is very good of you."

"It is what sisters do for one another. Perhaps you might be able to take me to her?"

How could he possibly do that when he did not know which room Miss Bennet occupied? But if he said yes, he could remain in her presence a little longer and try to capture her likeness with surreptitious glances. "Pray, come with me."

After leaving her in the care of the housekeeper, he joined Bingley and his sisters in the parlor. With any luck, Miss Elizabeth might call upon them before she left Netherfield. A few more moments to memorize her features was worth the small talk. It would not be enough, to be sure, but it was something.

———◦✧◦———

Not only did Providence smile upon him, but it outright waved its banner and sang joyous airs over him. Miss Bennet was too sick to be moved, and her sister insisted upon staying with her. To be sure, he could not rejoice that the other young lady was ill, and he would certainly mourn and perhaps even feel guilty if her condition took a turn for the worse. But the opportunity to share the same house with Miss Elizabeth and fix her features into his mind's eye was too great a boon to leave unappreciated.

No doubt fortune would extract a heavy price for her favor, but for now he would bask in its glow.

The following morning, he remained in the morning room until Miss Elizabeth made a brief appearance to break her fast. Quite conveniently, the room had been established on the east side of the house, allowing the best of the morning sunlight to filter in through gauzy white curtains. The furnishings, though older and a bit heavy, did not clutter the space, leaving it conveniently without visual impediments.

Since Miss Elizabeth chose to read, he took advantage of her preoccupation to study the perfect asymmetry of her face. Though aesthetics dictated perfect symmetry to be ideal in any woman, it was her slight imperfections—almost too slight to notice— that made her so intriguing, so utterly delightful: the singular dimple on her right cheek; the tiny cleft in her chin, just slightly to the right as well; the tiny beauty mark on her left cheek.

And her eyes. To say they were merely "fine"—as Miss Bingley had mockingly called them—would be to insult them. They were exquisite, dark and deep with feeling and intelligence. Worthy of a study of their own.

So worthy, in fact, thereafter he took to bringing his journal to the morning room to sketch her eyes while he sipped his coffee. Since it was only eyes and nothing more, he could easily claim they were a general sort of study, not his record against a future without her as a direct reference. Oh, how that thought stung, like a slice to his soul.

Best refrain from considering it whilst she was here, now, in the flesh, lest he fail to use this rare opportunity to its fullest.

In the evenings after dinner, she would join them for at least a little while in the drawing room. There she often read, offering him yet another unparalleled opportunity to record her profile, her expressions in his thoughts and his sketchbook. Perhaps now that Miss Bennet was recovering a bit, she would stay there with him—and the rest of the house party— longer.

Fortune smiled on him once more in the form of Miss Bennet's recovery which brought both young ladies to the drawing room that night. Gracious, in what manner would payment be exacted for this blessing? No doubt the cost would be dear—but whatever it was, it would be worthwhile.

Darcy lingered in the hallway between the dining room and the drawing room. Watching Miss Elizabeth walk, studying her grace, her motion, was something not to be missed. She guided her sister into the drawing room, most solicitous of Miss Bennet's comfort, seeing her well-guarded from cold and draft, conversing with Bingley's sisters. Odd, though, how Miss Bingley's attentions seemed to immediately shift toward him when he, Bingley, and Hurst entered the room.

Though some would insist Miss Bingley's powers of conversation were considerable, they always felt more like a performance than an actual interpersonal engagement, making them somewhat off-putting. But, then again, many such engagements were off-putting themselves, so perhaps it really was not indicative of very much.

Bingley immediately sought to make himself useful to Miss Bennet. He spent the first half hour piling up the fire lest she should suffer from the cold. At his desire, she moved to the other side of the fireplace that she might be farther from the door and its dreadful drafts. Then he sat down by her and scarcely talked to anyone else. If a man could have been more attentive, it was difficult to imagine. Miss Elizabeth, at her needlework in the opposite corner, saw it all with shining eyes.

While Bingley's display was mawkish at best, it did

provide Darcy with the most enchanting expression of Miss Elizabeth's to capture. Such joy, just pure happiness. Had he ever seen such affection carried only in the eyes? He pulled out his pocket sketchbook and set to work with his pencil. He could not afford to forget any detail of the lady's quiet delight and enchantment.

It said a great deal about Miss Elizabeth's character that she could show such quiet joy for her sister without any trace of jealousy on her own behalf. Yes, that was a very pleasing trait in a woman—a beautiful one. He jotted a small note to himself to that effect. Sometimes it was useful to know what his models were thinking as he painted them. Somehow it made the expressions more engaging.

But truly, what was she thinking? Why was she happy for her sister? Was it the very advantageous nature of a match with Bingley? Certainly, that would be what her mother would suggest. Perhaps it was best not to continue thinking along those lines.

"I say, Mr. Darcy, I cannot make it out from here. Are you reading or are you writing—or is it drawing that you are about?" Miss Bingley looked up from her book and stared at him. She probably had not even been reading it in the first place. She hardly seemed the type intent upon improving her mind in such a way

"I often find it helpful to make notes for future reference." He returned to his sketch. Was Miss Bingley quick enough to realize he had offered no answer to her question?

The tiny dimple that creased Miss Elizabeth's cheek suggested she was.

"How pleasant it is to spend an evening in this

way! I declare, after all there is no enjoyment like reading! How much sooner one tires of anything other than of a book! When I have a house of my own, I shall be miserable if I have not an excellent library." Miss Bingley shut her book rather loudly.

Darcy clamped his jaws shut. The thought of Miss Bingley refusing a suitor on the count of an insufficient library was one of the few things funny enough to make him want to laugh aloud.

From near the fireplace, Bingley's voice rose just enough for the rest of the room to hear. "I do so love a ball."

Miss Bingley leaned back and looked over her shoulder at Bingley. "By the bye, Charles, are you really serious in considering a dance at Netherfield? I would advise you, before you determine on it, to consult the wishes of the present party. I am much mistaken if there are not some among us to whom a ball would be rather a punishment than a pleasure."

Bingley sought Darcy's gaze and rolled his eyes. "If you mean Darcy, he may go to bed before it begins, if he chooses—but as for the ball, it is quite a settled thing. As soon as Nicholls has made white soup enough, I shall send round my cards."

Miss Bingley looked directly at Darcy. "I should like balls infinitely better, if they were carried on in a different manner; but there is something insufferably tedious in the usual process of such a meeting. It would surely be much more rational if conversation instead of dancing were the order of the day."

Had Miss Bingley any idea of how ridiculous she sounded? Something in the way Miss Elizabeth hid a dainty cough in her hand suggested that she might.

"Much more rational, my dear Caroline, I dare say,

but it would not be near so much like a ball."

Miss Bingley's eyes darted about as though she were looking for some sort of retort, but finding none, she got up and walked about the room. Her figure was elegant, and she walked well enough, but hardly enough out of the ordinary to be worth taking note. If ever he needed to render such a character, he could find her kind aplenty in any assembly in London.

She meandered across the room. "Miss Eliza Bennet, let me persuade you to follow my example, and take a turn about the room. I assure you it is very refreshing after sitting so long in one attitude."

Elizabeth glanced at Darcy and agreed. No, it was not possible that she understood his deepest desire and was acceding to it, was it? No, it could not be. Providence was pouring out all it had upon him.

"Would you care to join us, Mr. Darcy?" Miss Bingley's eyebrow arched suggestively.

And lose this opportunity to observe? "I must decline. I can imagine but two motives for your choosing to walk up and down the room together, with either of which motives my joining you would interfere."

Miss Bingley leaned in close to Miss Elizabeth. "What could he mean? I am dying to know what could be his meaning"

"Depend upon it, he means to be severe on us, and our surest way of disappointing him will be to ask nothing about it." Miss Elizabeth turned her face aside and tried to walk on, but Miss Bingley retarded her progress.

"No, no, I insist upon knowing. Mr. Darcy, do explain yourself."

He leaned forward, closing his sketchbook. "I have not the smallest objection to explaining. You either choose this method of passing the evening because you are in each other's confidence and have secret affairs to discuss, or because you are conscious that your figures appear to the greatest advantage in walking. If the first, I should be completely in your way, and if the second, I can admire you much better as I sit by the fire." He returned to his sketchbook to commit his admiration to paper before he lost this unique approbation to stare at them as much as he cared.

After all, how many times did such an opportunity come to one? He dare not allow a moment of it to be missed.

Miss Bingley gasped and stared at him. "Oh! shocking! I never heard anything so abominable. How shall we punish him for such a speech?"

"Nothing so easy, if you have but the inclination," Elizabeth glanced back at him, her eyes gaining a heretofore unseen fire. "Tease him; laugh at him. Intimate as you are, you must know how it is to be done."

Spectacular! She was spectacular!

"But upon my honor I do not. I do assure you that my intimacy has not yet taught me that." Miss Bingley pressed her hand to her chest. Her bulging eyes suggested she was truly surprised as he had never seen her before. "Tease calmness of temper and presence of mind! No, no—I feel he may defy us there. And as to laughter, we will not expose ourselves, if you please, by attempting to laugh without a subject."

"Mr. Darcy is not to be laughed at! That is an uncommon advantage, and uncommon I hope it will continue, for it would be a great loss to me to have many such acquaintances. I dearly love a laugh." A musical laugh followed as if to prove a point.

Was it possible to capture such a sound in paint?

He cleared his throat. "Miss Bingley has given me credit for more than can be. The wisest and the best of men, nay, the wisest and best of their actions, may be rendered ridiculous by a person whose first object in life is a joke."

Elizabeth turned away from Miss Bingley and faced him directly. "Certainly, there are such people, but I hope I am not one of them. I hope I never ridicule what is wise or good. Follies and nonsense, whims and inconsistencies do divert me, I own, and I laugh at them whenever I can. But these, I suppose, are precisely what you are without."

How could one resist the challenge, the flame in her eyes, the pointedness of her voice? He leaned toward her. "Perhaps that is not possible for anyone. But it has been the study of my life to avoid those weaknesses which often expose a strong understanding to ridicule."

"Such as vanity and pride."

"Yes, vanity is a weakness indeed. But pride— where there is a real superiority of mind, pride will be always under good regulation."

Elizabeth turned away to hide a smile. Whatever did she mean by that? Did she agree with his statement, or did she find it somehow amusing and laughable? Would he ever know?

"Your examination of Mr. Darcy is over, I presume, and pray what is the result?" Miss Bingley's voice took on an uneasy edge.

"I am perfectly convinced by it that Mr. Darcy has no defect. He owns it himself without disguise." Miss Elizabeth's gaze remained fixed on him.

"No," Darcy stood—did not one rise when challenged? His heart beat a little faster—who would have suspected his muse had such wit? "I have made no such pretension. I have faults enough, but they are not, I hope, of understanding. My temper, I dare not vouch for. It is, I believe, too little yielding, certainly too little for the convenience of the world. I cannot forget the follies and vices of others so soon as I ought, nor their offences against myself. My feelings are not puffed about with every attempt to move them. My temper would perhaps be called resentful. My good opinion once lost is lost forever."

Gracious, why had he said that? Why had he said any of it? He never talked of himself and certainly never in such a way!

"That is a failing indeed! Implacable resentment is a shade in a character." Miss Elizabeth folded her arms over her chest, frost tinging her voice. "But you have chosen your fault well. I really cannot laugh at it. You are safe from me."

"There is, I believe, in every disposition a tendency to some particular evil, a natural defect which not even the best education can overcome." Why could he not give up this conversation?

"And your defect is a propensity to hate everybody."

"And yours is willfully to misunderstand them." His face flushed, and his breath came a little faster. No one, particularly a woman, had ever spoken to him so.

"Do let us have a little music." Miss Bingley harrumphed and hurried to the pianoforte.

The instrument was opened, and Darcy returned to his sketches. It took all his strength not to look at her, not to stare and study the fiery goddess before him, but one did not stare at such a figure without getting burned.

Perhaps it was too late already. Perhaps this was the price of the muse's favor: the danger of paying Miss Elizabeth too much attention.

⸺⚸⸺

The ensuing fortnight sent Darcy—or rather his muse—into a frenzy. In the midst of it all, he assured himself that he was, in fact, in control of the entire process but intentionally chose to give into his creative instincts.

Bingley argued that Darcy was hardly in control of anything.

None of it mattered in the fervor of creative productivity. Every moment of daylight, Darcy painted. In the candlelight of evening, he sketched references to stay him against the inevitable removal from Miss Elizabeth's presence. Nearly every aspect of her person, her eyes, her ears, her fingers, even her elbow were all added to that valuable compendium.

Miss Bingley had seen it once. She thought it rather dear how artists like he and Bingley were forever scratching away in their books, sketching this and that but never really finishing much. Worse yet, in her vanity, she was complimented to think that it might be herself figuring in those sketches. He did not bother to correct her.

Chapter 2

DARCY STOOD BEFORE his mirror. His valet had left moments before, having tied Darcy's finely starched cravat in an intricate knot. There was a certain art to getting those things just right. One could become obsessed with it if he allowed himself.

On more than one occasion, Darcy had been told that he cut a dashing figure and ought to paint a likeness of himself. After all, he despised all the attempts made by the artists his father had hired. The notion was flattering, but it would never happen.

Hours spent staring at himself in a mirror—what an utterly depressing thought. He was no artists' model. His features were too irregular—or at least they were to his practiced eye. His expressions were decidedly dour, no matter how he tried to school them otherwise. No, he would rather paint beauty.

He would rather paint Miss Elizabeth.

And shortly he would see her. Tonight, at the ball.

Although he put on the expected show of disliking the social convention for Miss Bingley's sake, mostly to prevent unnecessary conversation, the truth was wildly different. His soul leapt at the opportunity to be with her again, to study her features, her expressions. In a ballroom, eye contact was accepted if not expected. He could stare at his partner and at the dancers in general, as much as he liked without raising an inquisitive eyebrow. Had he only taken the opportunity at the Meryton Assembly, tonight's event might not feel like air to a drowning man. But he did not know then what he knew now: his muse had taken the form of that particular young woman. Tonight, he would not waste the opportunity.

By the time he made it downstairs, guests had already begun to arrive. Since he was not part of the family, he could avoid the greeting line and discreetly watch arrivals. Each one told a story; each figure painted a tale in his mind. Though none were as interesting as Miss Elizabeth, he strove to capture each one for future reference.

Sir William Lucas trundled in, his wife in tow. His suit was new, his wife's dress not—the sort of thing a woman wore when all her resources were being utilized on daughters on the marriage mart. That he wore a new garment spoke something of his character—and it was hardly complimentary. Still though, the way people greeted him suggested he was well thought of in his local company. He did not appear at ease, though, clearly bewildered as to how exactly to behave in a place where his knighthood was eclipsed by substantial wealth.

A family called Goulding arrived with several young people, all eager to show off their accomplishments to a crowd that might include better company than they were accustomed to. The eager, wistful light in the girls' eyes was worth capturing in a sketch later … as long as that look did not get turned on him. Perhaps he ought to avoid close observation of that family lest he seem to invite their attention.

Someone said the name Bennet, and his focus was immediately fixed on the entry. Yes, there she was. In white muslin, of course, for her family could not have afforded silk. Her figure would be astonishing draped in white silk. Perhaps it was best it was not. The gauzy white muslin was quite enough to negate the possibility of tearing his eyes away from her.

She glanced in his direction. While his heart pinched at her look of annoyance, his artist's eye seized upon the exquisite turn of her lips, the spark in her eyes, the angle at which she held her head. Oh, to be able to commit her image to paper just now. He stared harder and longer to make sure he would never forget.

Impatience demanded he ask her for the first two dances. But, unfortunately, discretion won the day. To ask so soon would suggest something that might be all too true, something he did not dare admit to, much less allow. No, he would dance with her, but not at the start. Besides, it seemed she was already claimed for those sets by Mr. Collins.

That man was an enigma to be sure. He was tall and well-made. Dressed appropriately to his station, not unpleasant to look at. That he was a vicar suggested he had some learning and might have some sense about him. Most university men were set apart that way.

But the impression did not survive this first encounter. One might easily surmise that his time at university had been ill-spent, learning only how to cater to those above him in hopes of acquiring a position. The kind of boot-licking sort of man who turned his stomach and made Darcy look for the nearest exit.

In some sense, the tendency might have served Collins well as it did secure Aunt Catherine's favor and the living she had to bestow. But outside of having obtained that living, there was little—or perhaps nothing—to be said in favor of the man and a great deal to be held against him.

The first item on that particular list of complaints was that the man could not dance. Fumble-footed did not begin to describe the ordeal poor Miss Elizabeth endured. Darcy would have felt her sufferance of Mr. Collins' ineptitude far more had it not afforded him a far greater range of expressions to admire than he had ever seen in her before. The look of determined self-control chiseled on her face was worth the whole uncomfortable episode. She might never agree, but sadly he probably would never have the opportunity to learn if she would if the matter were explained. Her expression of ecstasy at her release from Collins was awe-inspiring as well but deeply uncomfortable.

Would that he experienced such an expression offered toward himself.

No, such thoughts were not at all helpful! Worse yet, they made watching her next dances with some nameless Meryton native exceedingly uneasy, even a mite wistful.

Thankfully, she did not dance the set after but

stood off to the side, speaking with her friend—Miss Lucas, was it? What confidences did she share with her friend? There was something in her stance that suggested her words were deeply felt.

Enough lingering and watching. He must go forth and take action now, lest the opportunity be utterly lost.

He tugged his jacket straight and strode toward Miss Elizabeth, guests parting in a wave before him.

Perhaps he had been abrupt; he spoke to her only long enough to obtain her hand for the next set, then walked away. He might have stayed; he should have stayed. He would have stayed had he felt any less. But in this moment of heady success, he did not dare reveal too much.

At the start of the next set, he sought her hand, his muse rendering him all but mute. To speak would distract from the minute observations which might be made in what could be a once-in-a-lifetime opportunity. He led her to the dance floor, enjoying the exquisite grace of her movements from the corner of his eye. She took her place across from him and waited rather expectantly.

What did she want?

"It is your turn to say something now, Mr. Darcy." Oh, the look of anticipation on her face! "I talked about the dance, and you ought to make some kind of remark on the size of the room, or the number of couples."

Of course, it was appropriate to make small talk at such a time as this. But what to say? On the canvas, he could communicate anything he desired, but words, particularly the spoken ones, were well beyond his skills. He swallowed hard. "Whatever you wish me to say should indeed be said."

"Very well. That reply will do for the present. Perhaps, by and by, I may observe that private balls are much pleasanter than public ones. But for now, we may be silent." She turned her face aside toward the other dancers.

She did not mean to ignore him, did she? Such punishment for merely being tongue-tied? No, absolutely not, it would not do. "Do you talk by rule, then, while you are dancing?"

"Sometimes. One must speak a little, you know. It would look odd to be entirely silent for half an hour together. Yet for the advantage of some, conversation ought to be so arranged that they may have the trouble of saying as little as possible." Her eyebrow arched just so—was she teasing him?

"Are you consulting your own feelings in the present case, or do you imagine that you are gratifying mine?" Blast and botheration, that sounded far sharper than he intended.

"Both, for I have always seen a great similarity in the turn of our minds. We are each of an unsocial, taciturn disposition, unwilling to speak unless we expect to say something that will amaze the whole room, and be handed down to posterity with all the éclat of a proverb."

"This is no very striking resemblance of your own character, I am sure. How near it may be to mine, I cannot pretend to say. You think it a faithful portrait undoubtedly." Did she really think those things of him, or was she teasing as he had seen her do often enough? Why did she demand of him a skill he would never possess?

Suddenly, it was their turn to join the dance, and

all opportunity to speak ceased. How gracefully she moved—with effortless vitality. To be entirely fair, she was hardly the best partner he had ever enjoyed, but there was something so fresh and lively in her steps, befitting the nymph of his paintings.

Finally, they reached the end of the line to wait out their turn. "Do you and your sisters often walk to Meryton?" That should be suitable conversation.

"Yes, we do. When you met us there the other day, we had just been forming a new acquaintance." Her brows arched as if to say far more than she spoke.

Yes, that day he had been to see Meryton's color-man. Whom had she been with—Wickham! His gut knotted, and all warmth drained from his face. If only she knew of the very great harm Wickham had done the Darcy family. But could such an innocent spirit as hers actually understand that level of intentional wickedness? How was he to make a response—one that her eyes clearly demanded? "Mr. Wickham is blessed with such happy manners as may ensure his making friends; whether he may be equally capable of retaining them is less certain."

"He has been so unlucky as to lose your friend-ship, and in a manner which he is likely to suffer from all his life." Her countenance declared she believed what she said.

She was so innocent and so easily and completely deceived. He clenched his jaw; best not to speak when all his words dripped venom.

Sir William Lucas suddenly appeared from the crowd. "I have been most highly gratified indeed, my dear sir. Such very superior dancing is not often seen. It is evident that you belong to the first circles. Allow me to say, however, that your fair partner does not disgrace you, and that I must hope to have this pleasure often repeated, especially when a certain desirable event, my dear Miss Eliza," he glanced at Miss Bennet and Bingley, "shall take place. What congratulations will then flow in! But let me not interrupt you, sir. You will not thank me for detaining you from the bewitching converse of that young lady whose bright eyes are also upbraiding me."

He was right. Miss Elizabeth looked utterly and entirely mortified. Not that she was without good reason; Sir William was crass—it seemed a common trait in this town. Even so, it pained him to see her so discomfited.

He glanced at the dance floor. Bingley was utterly entranced with his partner, and Miss Bennet seemed to bear it well. She was a beauty, to be sure, but far less interesting than her sister—whom he had now been ignoring whilst he stared at his friend. "Sir William's interruption has made me forget what we were talking of."

"I do not think we were speaking at all. Sir William could not have interrupted any two people in the room who had less to say for themselves. We have tried two or three subjects already without success, and what we are to talk of next I cannot imagine." Her eyes glinted with the absurdity she suggested.

"What think you of books?" Surely, she could not fault that question.

"Books? Oh no! I am sure we never read the same, or not with the same feelings."

"I am sorry you think so; but if that be the case, there can at least be no want of subject. We may compare our different opinions."

"No." Her laugh was truly musical. "I cannot talk

of books in a ballroom; my head is always full of something else."

"The present always occupies you in such scenes, does it?" Might she be about to reveal something telling about her deepest self?

"Yes, always." She looked away, clearly lost in other musings. She turned back to him abruptly, eyes just a mite narrowed. "I remember hearing you once say that you hardly ever forgave, that your resentment once created was unappeasable. You are very cautious, I suppose, as to its being created."

She would remember that conversation just now. "I am."

"And never allow yourself to be blinded by prejudice?"

"I hope not." He swallowed hard against his suddenly too-tight cravat.

"It is particularly incumbent on those who never change their opinion to be secure of judging properly at first." She met his gaze with an intense one of her own.

"May I ask to what these questions tend?"

"Merely to the illustration of your character. I am trying to make it out." Her eyebrows flashed up as her shoulders lifted.

His cheeks grew hot. "And what is your success?"

"I do not get on at all. I hear such different accounts of you as puzzle me exceedingly." She shook her head.

"I can readily believe the report of my character may vary greatly with respect to me. I could wish, Miss Bennet, that you were not to sketch my character at the present moment, as there is reason to fear that the performance would reflect no credit on either." Was it too much to hope she would understand?

"But if I do not take your likeness now, I may never have another opportunity."

"I would by no means suspend any pleasure of yours." Perhaps it was a mercy that the dance had come to an end. It would not do for her to try to take his likeness when every artist who had tried failed.

He escorted her from the dance floor and left her in the company of Miss Bingley.

Though a relief, the parting also brought with it a poignant soul ache, nearly physical in its intensity.

No, this was not good at all. His powerful feelings toward this woman were a very bad sign, indeed. One did not feel this way toward a muse. It was sure to be more of a hinderance than a help. As were the very negative sensations he felt toward one Mr. Wickham. Perhaps, just perhaps, his muse would be satisfied now, and he could rest—somewhere well away from Hertfordshire.

———⚜———

Bingley had business in London just after the ball, so he left the next day. Odd for him to be so close-lipped about his intentions; usually, he was quite free with such information. But perhaps that was good as it offered Darcy a ready excuse to follow him to London.

But he could not, would not, go back to that county again. That Bennet woman was difficult enough to leave behind—not to mention her sympathies for Wickham were not to be borne. He could not risk becoming caught in her orbit. If that happened, he might never leave … something he dare not risk.

Truly, it was for the best.

⚜

A week after his return to London, the Hursts invited him to dine with them, Bingley, and Miss Bingley. Since he was in the midst of a project, he would ordinarily have refused the offer. But there was something not quite right about the composition, and a little time away might help his perspective, so he dressed and presented himself at Hurst's townhouse at the requisite date and time.

The butler led him down the finely appointed corridor—the Hursts' taste was better than one might expect, given the man's manners—to the drawing room where Miss Bingley, and only Miss Bingley, awaited him.

The back of his neck prickled as he made certain the door was not closed behind him. He forced a calm expression though he felt like a cornered rat.

"Good evening, Mr. Darcy." She rose from the center of the white sofa and curtsied. Her pale blue silk skirts rippled and flowed with the movement, like the calm waters of a stream running in its course.

"Miss Bingley." He sat down, choosing the chair second most distant from her—a rather uncomfortable ivory and blue bergère that was wrong for his frame in every dimension. The legs were too short, the armrests too high. The seat cushion was too soft and the back overstuffed. In short, sitting in it was a miserable experience. But it was necessary; she was the type of woman to easily get the wrong idea, and everything about the current situation suggested she very much wanted to do just that. While she was not nearly so dreadful an option as marrying his cousin,

Anne, Miss Bingley was hardly a marriageable sort.

No, that was hardly true; she was exactly the marriageable sort. And that was the problem. Miss Bingley was a woman with a large dowry and excellent accomplishments who could infuse cash into a floundering estate. That sort of exchange went on all the time, with both parties walking away satisfied: the gentleman with his estate supported, she with an entry into the gentry and all the respectability that came with it.

Exactly the sort of business arrangement he neither wanted nor needed.

"I hope you will forgive me for suggesting you arrive slightly earlier than perhaps my brothers and sister were prepared for." She returned to her seat, folded her hands in her lap, and posed like a model sitting for a portrait.

Was that her intention? She would not be the first to try to drop hints to him. It was so difficult to tell with this woman. The backdrop of the room, neatly and elegantly decorated with just enough color to please the eye but not so much as to be jarring, felt natural enough. Perhaps she was not hinting that he should take her likeness.

"I had hoped that I might have a few private words with you before Charles comes down." Her gaze flickered toward the doorway.

Private words? His chest tightened. "Go on."

"I am so worried about him. I fear he might be in grave danger of making some serious mistakes." Her brow knit just enough to show concern but not so much as to be unattractive.

Was that expression something she had learnt in school? It seemed like the sort of thing that might be taught as it was hardly natural. How many times had he needed to school a model on getting just the right balance?

"What sort of error? Is he contemplating some sort of business he has not told me about?" Bingley had been rather more secretive recently.

"Not to my knowledge, but that is hardly the sort of thing that he discusses with me." She looked down at her hands. "There are other serious mistakes that a man like him might make."

"Such as?"

"The business of marriage."

"Marriage? He has said nothing to me of such a thing. I am certain he would discuss such a step with me before he took it." He would be a fool if he did not. Bingley was in no position for society to forgive him a significant social blunder—such as marrying the wrong sort of woman.

"I have no doubt that he would—that he will when such a time comes. And to be clear, I do not believe that we are at that point—at least not yet. But it is possible that it could come far sooner than it should. In fact, I would like to keep it from coming to that point in the near future."

He muttered under his breath and frowned. "You will have to speak more plainly. I do not pretend to understand what you are speaking of."

"Miss Bennet of Longbourn."

No, no! Not that name—Bennet!

"You agree with me. I can see it on your face. I am so relieved; I cannot tell you how much."

How dare she believe she understood what he was thinking. The addlepate knew nothing! "What are you inferring?"

"You cannot believe Charles should marry Miss Bennet."

"I did not think he was currently contemplating marriage to anyone."

"Charles is always contemplating marriage, I am afraid. As much as women might be accused of being overly romantic, I fear Charles is just as bad or even worse." She pressed her hand to her chest and sucked in a sorrowful breath.

Melodramatic overreaction. It was neither attractive nor effective.

"He is a sensible man."

"He can be made to see sense, that I will concede." She tipped her head toward him, eyes batting the slightest bit like butterflies taking their rest.

Butterflies were never so calculated.

"You seem to be hinting that you want something from me." He pinched the bridge of his nose.

"After a fashion, I do. I need to beg a favor of you."

Darcy clenched his jaw. Doing favors for women, particularly women like her, was not likely to go well for him in the long run.

She leaned toward him slightly. "Pray help me to make sure that Charles stays away from Miss Bennet so there is no chance of any further attachment occurring."

"I am not in favor of such subterfuge. Disguise is my abhorrence."

"I do not much like it myself, but what choice is there?"

"I believe, in these matters, it is better to be direct. Explain your concerns to him—"

She sat up very straight, her eyebrows lifting high

on her forehead as her tone rose to meet them. "Explain my concerns? Surely you jest! That is the surest possible way to see that he does exactly what I am certain he should not! The mere mention of it will place the idea in the forefront of his imagination, and he will hardly think about anything else until he acts upon it."

"You do not appear to have a high estimation of your brother." Unfortunately, though, she was right.

"You wound me. You know I think a very great deal of him. But I am also aware of his weaknesses. Think just a bit about the matter. How many times has he discovered a new 'angel' among an assembly or a party? You know it is very frequent. As often as he changes company, he finds a beautiful face and figure and falls enamored of her."

Darcy rubbed his fist along his chin. She did have an excellent point.

"Who is to say that Miss Bennet is not another one of these women? You have seen how once he is out of their company, his infatuation fades, and all returns to how it had been."

At least it had been so in every instance to date.

"Tell me, how firm an attachment could he have made to any of these girls if he forgets about them once they are out of sight?" She extended her hand, inviting him to agree.

He murmured under his breath. Another good point.

"I am quite certain that if he is attached to her, he cannot forget her, certainly not so easily as by discouraging his return to Hertfordshire. I will not be disingenuous with him."

"I am not asking you to." She pressed her hands

into the sofa beside her. "But you cannot tell me you think Miss Bennet an excellent match for him."

He looked aside. "She has many fine qualities. He is not in need of a dowry, and her father is a gentleman."

"I grant you that, but her family, her connections? Can you tell me they are in any way acceptable? Her mother, her youngest sisters, they are horrid! I still shudder to think of them at the ball. The mother intimating they were nearly engaged, and the youngest girl cavorting with the officers."

Miss Elizabeth was not—

"Can you honestly tell me that you think those are the sort of connections that will serve Charles well?"

He covered his eyes with his hand. "I can see some difficulties."

"Then you will assist me?"

"I am willing to support your notion that some time apart cannot be a bad thing." And it meant that Bingley would not be pushing him to return to Hertfordshire which would be a good thing.

"Indeed, that is all I am asking … Charles, there you are! I had wondered if you were feeling unwell!" She rose and met her brother in the doorway.

It should not have been surprising that Bingley was, at least at first, reluctant to accept the helpful suggestions offered by Miss Bingley. Only when Darcy chimed in with his support did Bingley finally give way and agree to remain in London. Miss Bingley rejoiced in her triumph as did Mrs. Hurst—her husband was generally too drunk to really care either way. But Bingley—his reaction was harder to read.

At first, he seemed sanguine about the notion, but soon thereafter the melancholy began, and he became the very essence of a brown study. Perhaps, just perhaps, Darcy had been mistaken.

Some weeks later, a visit to Bingley had seemed like a good idea. A reasonable one at least. What harm was there in trying to visit his friend and perhaps cheer him up just a bit? Darcy had hoped to study Bingley again and perhaps even recant his position. Returning to Netherfield might not be the evil Caroline suggested it was if leaving Hertfordshire had left Bingley in such a state.

But Darcy had been wrong—about all of it.

He dashed into his own townhouse, up the stairs, and locked the door of his chambers behind him. Panting, he pressed his back against the door—perhaps that would keep the tormenting spirits at bay.

He had seen her, Miss Bennet—the wrong Miss Bennet—waiting at the door at Grosvenor Street only to be sent away by the butler, told that Miss Bingley was not at home. Her face when she had turned aside was so composed, so serene. How could she possibly actually have any fondness for Bingley when she was so untouched by being turned away at their door?

But still, there was something about the cast of her shoulders, the turn of her lips that suggested she might be more moved than she appeared at first glance. If it had been Miss Elizabeth, he would have been certain of the meaning of her expression. With this wrong Miss Bennet, he could only guess. And her eyes…oh how they resembled Miss Elizabeth's.

Not so much in the delicacy of that feature but in rough form and color. Almost as though she were a rough draft of what was to be perfected in her sister.

Of all that was so perfectly imperfect in Miss Elizabeth.

Her face, her figure whirled though the shadows of his imagination twirling her, parading her before his mind's eye--the nymph who lived to tease and torment him in turn.

Unfortunately, Miss Bingley was right in regard to the Bennets. While Bingley could technically afford an alliance with Longbourn, Miss Elizabeth was everything a man like himself should, must, was even required to, avoid.

He would respect his family and his station enough for that, his muse be damned. He would not tell Bingley of Miss Bennet's visit, nor that she was even in London. And he certainly would never, never recommend a return to Netherfield Park.

.

Chapter 3

WHY WAS IT his muse had seemed to take the notion to be "damned" far more literally than it should have? No sooner did he return to his paints but every fragment, every thread of inspiration flew from him, as fleeting as a shadow and as easy to catch when he gave it chase.

He tried the theater, the opera, reading, riding Rotten Row, even walking in any green space he found, but all creative impulse eluded him. After a fortnight, the futility of it all set in, and he retreated back to Derbyshire. If he was going to be miserable, he might as well do it in comfortable surroundings.

———✦———

At first, the return to Pemberley helped. After an extended time away, accumulated estate business kept him gainfully occupied for a solid month. What a month it was! One of occupation of mind, of useful engagements and meaningful activities.

In some ways, mundane in the fullest sense of the word, but in others, truly and absolutely glorious. Every meeting with his steward, every call from a tenant with complaints proved welcome in a way it never had before. The aching, incessant weight of his muse faded away in favor of useful, practical employment.

Blissful.

And over far too soon.

By the beginning of February, his paints and brushes, his pencils and crayons—anything with which he could make a mark—began to call him again. A whisper at first, but the volume increased steadily. Only a fortnight's resistance was permitted before he was drawn back to his attic studio to confront half-finished works and a tormenting blank canvas.

Initially, the unfinished works proved a balm, giving him a place to start, a direction to go, freeing him from those first, sometimes awful decisions that were demanded in the first moments of creation. When his muse proved temperamental, she delighted to torture him in that critical initial period. Was it wrong to delight in thwarting her efforts?

But even that reprieve was not to last. Another fortnight saw all the unfinished pieces completed—not to his satisfaction, but completed. A landscape copied from one of John Constable's works that he had seen at the Royal Academy, the image of his favorite pointer—what had possessed him to paint that?—a still life of his mother's favorite things—a bit too sentimental and heart-stirring to truly enjoy—and the view from the studio windows of his favorite spot in the river where he and his father often fished, so long ago now. All of those had been begun before he left Pemberley for Bingley's company in London though, and hardly fulfilled the maddening drive now consuming him.

With no works left to finish, he confronted a blank canvas. Shapes began to take form one after another, but damn it all, they were all extensions of his study of the nymph in the forest. This time, though, her face took shape. The face of Elizabeth Bennet. Every single time.

This had to stop! It simply had to stop! Such unwarranted intrusion upon his mind and art was not to be borne! How dare she? How dare she!

So, he tried to paint Caroline Bingley's visage instead. Disaster, unmitigated disaster. She was no nymph. She was a siren, somehow confined to land—resentful of her limited existence and her fate. Her beauty, such as it was, and her song would only lead a man to his death.

That particular canvas offended his own sensibilities and his muse so much that there was little choice but to burn it, lest he never sleep another night.

Aunt Catherine's summons for his annual Easter visit to Rosings Park came as a relief though it would not likely remain so once he arrived and the demands to marry Anne began anew. Still, it was better than pacing his studio whilst his muse continued to torment him.

The journey to Kent proved nothing like the ride to Hertfordshire. Nothing. And yet, the promise of a journey was all it took to send his muse thrumming, awakening every nerve with agonizing precision.

It was not possible, but still his ears ached for Miss Elizabeth's musical voice; his eyes sought her in every shadow, every flash of sunlight. He longed for the scent of her—what sort of flower was it that she wore? All hunger, yet knowing no satisfaction awaited him at the end of this journey. That should have been enough to quell the longing, but no, somehow it only increased the anticipation. It only served to make the disappointment when he saw Anne all the more acute.

Realistically, he should look forward to that. The sight of Anne was enough to chill his muse into silence. Usually. But not this time.

But why?

Why could he not cease to hear Miss Elizabeth's voice on the wind, see her face in fleeting shimmers of light? Why had he come here at all? Dreadful fool he was to think he could flee the relentless cur nipping at the heels of his soul.

He locked himself in his room with the curtains drawn against the sun. Perhaps he could sleep until it was time to depart this horrible place.

Fitzwilliam insisted he drag himself to Holy Services on Sunday. While it was his habit to do so, the knowledge that the vicar was none other than Miss Elizabeth's cousin made the entire affair unpalatable at best. But after Fitzwilliam's years in the army, he could be a force to be reckoned with, and Darcy lacked the energy for the standoff. Thus, he went.

Though the sun was bright and the air crisp and fresh, the walk to the stone parish church was flat and dull and grey. The birdsong seemed monotone and off-key; even the bleating of sheep rasped harshly against his beleaguered nerves.

The smell of cold, damp stone filled his nostrils as he settled into the family pew, trying to avoid eye contact. Yes, there were those with whom he shared an acquaintance, and he should deign to speak with them. He would fulfill all the obligations of etiquette at the first moment that civility was available to him. For now, it was not.

A flash of blue caught his eye. His lungs seized and refused to breathe.

Wait. No, it could not be. It was simply not possible. There in the vicar's family pew with a woman who must be Mrs. Collins.

Her.

Darcy swallowed hard and blinked several times. Breathe, he must breathe.

"Darcy? Darcy? Are you well? You look like you have seen the devil himself." Fitzwilliam elbowed him sharply.

Darcy jumped and shook his head. "Yes, yes, I am fine."

"You have noticed Mrs. Collins' houseguests, I see. Aunt Catherine was just telling me about them."

Them? Were there two? By Jove, yes there were two young ladies sitting with Mrs. Collins. One must be her sister; they shared a very similar look. But the other—

"… the other is Miss Elizabeth Bennet, I am told, a childhood friend of Mrs. Collins and cousin of Mr. Collins."

His heart swelled to fill all his chest and shut off any hope of breathing. It was her—it was her! Here in the middle of exactly where she had no reason, no hope of being, she was here. A strange sense overtook him. A foreign mix of peace and euphoria floated his limbs and left his head muzzy and light.

The next day, he lost no time in suggesting to Fitzwilliam that it would only be proper for them to pay a call upon the parsonage to honor the new Mrs. Collins. While Fitzwilliam raised an eyebrow at the suggestion, he did not hesitate to act upon any idea that would excuse them from Aunt Catherine's presence.

And no wonder. Aunt Catherine was in rare form this visit. Even in the short time they had been there, she had wasted no time in insisting that Darcy act upon hers and his mother's plans for their offspring to wed. While it would be a sure way to silence his muse forever, he was not yet that desperate. Still, a shiver snaked down his back as he trotted downstairs, avoiding the parlor Aunt Catherine preferred to use in the mornings.

Darcy had been in the parsonage often enough; he and Fitzwilliam always called there when they visited Rosings Park. The prior vicar had not been dissimilar to Mr. Collins, grateful for Aunt Catherine's condescension and a bit of a toad-eater—probably the basis by which Aunt Catherine chose the current holder of the living.

But somehow the place felt different as the housekeeper showed them in. It was not the lighting, nor was it the smell. A presence—sweet and steady—filled the entire house, noticeable the moment he entered the front door. She was indeed here.

Mrs. Collins—had he met her before? She seemed familiar—they must have met in Hertfordshire. That was it! He had seen her at the Netherfield Ball. A plain, mousy woman, exactly the sort that would have married the vicar, she introduced Fitzwilliam to Miss Elizabeth who curtsied to them both, saying nothing.

But she did not need to say a single word. Her presence spoke everything that needed to be said. The previously unremarkable parlor sang with her being, and his muse sang harmony against its melody.

How could he be so supremely favored to find her here when his soul was the most desperate? What would such favor cost him?

Fitzwilliam prattled on for some time with the readiness and ease of a well-bred man. Darcy exhausted his conversation after having addressed a minor observation on the house and garden to Mrs. Collins.

It might not have been noteworthy conversation, but it was sufficient to be considered polite. More important, it permitted him to remain and allow his muse to nourish itself with sidelong glances at its sustenance. Perhaps he could, he should, force himself to say something more. "Is your family in good health, Miss Bennet?"

"They are, thank you. My eldest sister has been in town these three months. Have you never happened to see her there?" Something about the way her brow arched as she looked at him.

His throat tightened so swiftly, he could not even exhale. He could not lie, but he could not tell her the manner in which he had seen the elder Miss Bennet. She required an answer, but how could he offer one? "I had not been so fortunate as to meet Miss Bennet in town."

It was entirely true; he had not lied. But something

about the way her eyes narrowed—how much more did she know, and how did she come to know it?

───※───

Those eyes preyed upon him, tortured him, taunted him with reminders of his subterfuge. But was not telling Bingley something that he would be better off not knowing truly wrong? Surely, it was for Bingley's own benefit that he concealed Miss Bennet's call. And his sister, her guilt was surely far more conspicuous. After all, she knew directly that Miss Bennet had come to the house; he had only happened upon her and surmised what had happened.

The logic was sound; his argument would have persuaded the king's finest barrister. But his muse was no barrister. She turned on him as surely as a vixen would turn on a threat to her kits. Was it possible for a muse to bare her teeth and growl, foaming at the mouth like a rabid dog? If it was, surely that was the sound that awakened him the next morning and every morning thereafter.

If only he could see Miss Bennet again, perhaps there would be some way he could make things right and appease his vengeful muse. But each time he tried to approach the parsonage, the image of her taut brow as her gaze penetrated his very being stopped him. Clearly, he could not intrude upon her solitude uninvited. So, he remained at Rosings manor, tortured, pacing his chambers like a caged wildcat, avoiding Aunt Catherine's demands.

Finally, after a full week had passed, the denizens of the parsonage were invited to Rosings Park to dine after church. Perhaps Aunt Catherine had grown weary of so little company; perhaps she thought their presence would draw Darcy out of his rooms. What-ever her reason, it meant that he could encounter her again and perhaps, somehow appease his muse's fury at his mistreatment of her chosen vessel.

Darcy presented himself in the drawing room a quarter of an hour prior to their guests' appointed arrival. The room was stiff and formal and largely purple, as it ever was, but the air crackled, electric in anticipation of the awaited company. Unfortunately, Aunt Catherine immediately seized upon him and Fitzwilliam for conversation.

Fitzwilliam handled it with aplomb, wandering away at the first opportunity to create a cozy cluster of chairs to draw their guests' companionship to him-self. Blast and botheration—did he realize what he was doing? He must—his posture gloated both over his triumph and the fact that Darcy could voice no complaint.

Their guests arrived, but only one mattered. She curtsied, greeted Aunt Catherine, and proceeded to join Fitzwilliam with her friend Mrs. Collins and Miss Lucas. Mr. Collins, naturally, waited upon his patron-ess.

What joy! Darcy's muse chittered something vengeful sounding in his ear—suggesting that perhaps he deserved this torment.

"You are on time tonight, I see, Mr. Collins." Did Aunt Catherine really need to state the obvious?

The vicar bowed, a glow of sweat simmering on his forehead. "Yes, your Ladyship. You have indeed impressed upon me—"

"And your guest, did you find she was apt to be

timely?" Aunt Catherine stared at Miss Elizabeth with a most peculiar, narrow-eyed look.

Mr. Collins sat in the stiff, polished chair nearest Aunt Catherine. "Yes, yes. She was most timely—"

"I am pleased to hear her mother has properly attended to those things."

Darcy hid his snort in a bout of coughing. If only Aunt Catherine knew Mrs. Bennet, she would never mistake good training having come from her. She was a dreadful influence on her daughters. It was a great credit to Miss Bennet and Miss Elizabeth that they were nothing like their mother.

Darcy's gaze wandered to the other side of the room. While their characters were utterly unalike, mother and daughter shared physical similarities. The lines of their jaws in particular favored one another. The shape of her cheeks and eyes were also similar. And their ears shared the same graceful curves and swirls. She had very attractive ears.

At some point in his sojourn to Hertfordshire, someone had mentioned that Mrs. Bennet had been a great beauty in her youth, and that was how she had got her husband. Her daughters were said to continue the line of family beauty. That was essentially correct, but to limit Miss Elizabeth's appearance in such a way was nearly criminal. Her beauty was hardly so ordinary.

Miss Elizabeth laughed—a lovely, light, lyrical sound—at something Fitzwilliam said. How vexing that he should be in conversation with her while Darcy could not. It did not help at all that Miss Elizabeth should smile and her eyes twinkle so over her merriment in Fitzwilliam's presence. Darcy's left hand balled into a fist.

"What is that you are saying, Fitzwilliam? What is it you are talking of? What are you telling Miss Bennet? Let me hear what it is." Aunt Catherine rapped her knuckles on the arm of her chair to punctuate her demands.

"We are speaking of music, madam." He glanced over his shoulder at her.

"Of music! Then pray speak aloud." She waved her boney hand, directing all attention towards herself as she eased back into her seat. "It is of all subjects my delight. I must have my share in the conversation if you are speaking of music. There are few people in England, I suppose, who have more true enjoyment of music than myself or a better natural taste. If I had ever learnt, I should have been a great proficient. And so would Anne, if her health had allowed her to apply. I am confident that she would have performed delightfully. How does Georgiana get on, Darcy?"

Darcy jumped. Aunt Catherine so rarely gave anyone else entry into the conversation, his mind went blank.

"Darcy?" And now she took offense at his lack of ready words. Delightful.

"I … uh … she is doing very well. She takes great joy in the instrument. I find her at practice many hours during the day. There is a new pianoforte being made ready for her even now. I believe it will bring her great pleasure to play on a superior instrument. Her music teachers have all reported that she is indeed a true proficient." It probably was not appropriate to bait his aunt so, but who could help themselves?

Fitzwilliam snorted into his hand.

"I am very glad to hear such a good account of

her," Aunt Catherine favored him with a small glower, "and pray tell her from me, that she cannot expect to excel if she does not practice a great deal."

Darcy gritted his teeth and drew two deep breaths before responding. "I assure you, madam, that she does not need such advice. She practices very constantly." That was decidedly impolite as he had already mentioned the scope of her practice.

"So much the better." She braced her elbows on the arms of her chair and pulled herself up very straight—a monarch issuing a decree. "It cannot be done too much, and when I next write to her, I shall charge her not to neglect it on any account. I often tell young ladies that no excellence in music is to be acquired without constant practice. I have told Miss Bennet…"

She had dared talk to Miss Bennet? No doubt insulted her, giving his muse more offense for him to atone for.

"… several times that she will never play really well unless she practices more, and though Mrs. Collins has no instrument, she is very welcome, as I have often told her, to come to Rosings every day, and play on the pianoforte in Mrs. Jenkinson's room. She would be in nobody's way, you know, in that part of the house."

Darcy winced and covered his face with his hand. Even if Aunt Catherine had not given prior offense, she was making the most of the opportunity now. Thankfully, a squadron of maids brought in refreshments, and Aunt Catherine was distracted, telling them precisely how to accomplish each task.

When coffee was over, Colonel Fitzwilliam reminded Miss Elizabeth of her promise to play for them. She sat down directly at the instrument, a picture of grace in each movement.

If there were ever an opportunity for him to move, it would be now. But how?

Fitzwilliam drew a chair near the pianoforte. Aunt Catherine listened to half a song, and then talked, far too loudly, to Darcy. Enough of her rudeness!

He walked away from her and quite deliberately to the pianoforte, stationing himself so as to command a full view of Elizabeth's astonishing countenance.

No, she was not a proficient musician; barely tolerable she would be considered in some circles. Her posture, according to Georgiana's music masters, was sloppy, and her hand position unacceptable. Still, she seemed to possess a muse of her own that lit her eyes and sweetened her voice as she played and sang for them.

Somehow, in some way utterly unexpected, one muse spoke to another and together they took flight, soaring above the confines of the floor, somewhere near the high ceiling above them. Dizzying, breathtaking, enchanting—

—and devastating as her music came to an abrupt halt.

She looked up at him, eyes full of lively fire. "You mean to frighten me, Mr. Darcy, by coming in all this state to hear me? But I will not be alarmed though your sister does play so well. There is a stubbornness about me that never can bear to be frightened at the will of others. My courage always rises with every attempt to intimidate me."

What state had he come to her in? Aching and empty, longing to be filled? Repentant and resolute to make reparations for his past wrongs? What did she think of him? "I shall not say that you are mistaken because you could not really believe me to entertain any design of alarming you. I have had the pleasure of your acquaintance long enough to know that you find great enjoyment in occasionally professing opinions which in fact are not your own."

Elizabeth laughed heartily.

The muses laughed with her.

Oh, how well that sounded! Surely that should count in his favor.

She turned to Fitzwilliam, color high in her cheeks. "Your cousin will give you a very pretty notion of me, and teach you not to believe a word I say. I am particularly unlucky in meeting with a person so well able to expose my real character in a part of the world where I had hoped to pass myself off with some degree of credit. Indeed, Mr. Darcy, it is very ungenerous of you to mention all that you knew to my disadvantage in Hertfordshire—and, give me leave to say, very impolitic too—for it is provoking me to retaliate, and such things may come out as will shock your relations to hear."

"I am not afraid of you." It was her disdain that he feared, not her teasing smiles and glittering eyes.

How difficult, profoundly difficult it was to tell what she was seeing in him right now. Damn it all! Why could he not read her easily? Why should others have that gift and not he?

"Pray let me hear what you have to accuse him of." Fitzwilliam leaned forward, elbows on his knees. "I should like to know how he behaves among strangers." He winked at Darcy.

"You shall hear then—but prepare yourself for something very dreadful. The first time of my ever seeing him in Hertfordshire, you must know, was at a ball—and at this ball, what do you think he did? He danced only four dances! I am sorry to pain you—but so it was. He danced only four dances, though gentlemen were scarce, and, to my certain knowledge, more than one young lady was sitting down in want of a partner. Mr. Darcy, you cannot deny the fact."

She had been one of those young ladies—that was bad enough—but that she should have also heard his unkind remarks as well! It was only just and fair that he should feel the sting of that now as much as she had then. No wonder his muse had been so profoundly offended. Was it telling that he had forgotten the incident? "I had not at that time the honor of knowing any lady in the assembly beyond my own party."

"True, and nobody can ever be introduced in a ball room." Her eyes held his with such just accusation that he could not look away.

He nodded very slowly, accepting the charges against him.

At last she looked aside. "Well, Colonel Fitzwilliam, what do I play next? My fingers wait your orders."

"Perhaps," Darcy cleared his throat softly, "I should have judged better and sought an introduction, but I am ill-qualified to recommend myself to strangers."

"Shall we ask your cousin the reason of this?" Her eyes flared with fresh fury. "Shall we ask him why a man of sense and education, and who has lived in the world, is ill-qualified to recommend himself to strangers?"

"I can answer your question without applying to

him." Fitzwilliam leaned back and crossed one leg over the other, his chair creaking softly. "It is because he will not give himself the trouble."

Darcy held his breath to keep from muttering. It was so good of Fitzwilliam to be such a staunch supporter, now that he was under such prosecution—just though it may be. "I certainly have not the talent which some people possess, of conversing easily with those I have never seen before. I cannot catch their tone of conversation, or appear interested in their concerns, as I often see done."

"My fingers," Elizabeth's eye brow arched just so, "do not move over this instrument in the masterly manner which I see so many women's do. They have not the same force or rapidity, and do not produce the same expression. But then, I have always supposed it to be my own fault—because I would not take the trouble of practicing. It is not that I do not believe my fingers as capable as any other woman's of superior execution. The fault is mine and mine alone."

Darcy forced a smile and nodded. "You are perfectly right. You have employed your time much better. No one admitted to the privilege of hearing you can think anything wanting. We neither of us perform to strangers."

She seemed to start at the notion that they were anything alike. That look of wonder and confusion in her eyes! If only he could get to his notebook quickly lest he forget it. The little crease between her brows that appeared when she was thinking formed. Was she now considering their similarities?

How compatible might two such people be? Would it not be very pleasing to have such a companion for his future life? His heart hammered staccato against his ribs.

"What are you talking of now? I must have my share in the conversation!" Aunt Catherine's shrill tones raised the hair on the back of his neck.

Miss Elizabeth immediately began playing, her muse taking his for a whirl about the room once again. Was it possible he had been forgiven? Could it be procured so easily: simply to allow her to tease against his foibles?

Aunt Catherine approached and listened for a few minutes. "Miss Bennet would not play at all amiss if she practiced more, and could have the advantage of a London master. She has a very good notion of fingering, though her taste is not equal to Anne's. Anne would have been a delightful performer, had her health allowed her to learn." Her tone warned, scolded him of the duty she believed he owed her.

Miss Elizabeth looked at him. Could she tell he did not agree with Aunt Catherine's continued litany of instructions on style, execution, and taste? Did she detect Aunt Catherine's real meaning? Oh, how Miss Elizabeth received the diatribe with all the forbearance of civility, even—at the request of Fitzwilliam—remaining at the instrument till her ladyship's carriage was ready to take them all home.

As he watched her disappear into the carriage, a stabbing ache lodged in his chest. Watching her depart was indeed a dreadful thing.

There had to be some way to make it stop.

***

The ache gave way to a cold void within, never easing, ever reminding him of the incompleteness.

That empty place within would only be quelled by time spent in her presence. But for that, he must pay a price.

His muse appeared satisfied with the offering of his pride upon her teasing altar, permitting, even encouraging, him to call upon the parsonage. This morning, not even the absence of Fitzwilliam would stop him from the pleasure his soul demanded as surely as it needed air. He hurried his valet though morning ablutions and made haste to the parsonage.

With every step toward his destination, only one purpose—that of filling the emptiness torn in him when Miss Bennet left Rosings Park—drew him. In her presence, there would be solace, wholeness once again. He composed himself briefly and rang the bell.

The maid guided him to the parlor to be greeted by Miss Elizabeth—and only Miss Elizabeth! What had he done to receive so great a privilege as to find her alone? He fought to catch his breath lest he greet his boon in stunned silence.

She rose and curtsied, the morning sunlight caressing her features. "Mr. Darcy! Pray excuse me, Mrs. Collins and Miss Lucas are gone to the village, and Mr. Collins has gone out on parish business."

"Forgive my intrusion, madam. I had thought all the ladies to be in this morning." He bowed from his shoulders. He should repine this situation; he should excuse himself from her presence. It was improper to be here alone with her, but his muse rooted his feet into place, and nothing was likely to enable him to move.

She stared at him for far too long, as if trying to make sense of the situation. "Pray, would you care to sit down?" She gestured at a chair—a rather ambivalent invitation to be sure, but it was enough.

But of course, it should be; she was a proper young lady in an improper situation.

If only his muse would agree and permit him to decline.

"Are Lady Catherine and her daughter well?" She sat down, her gown falling into graceful folds in the sunbeam that enveloped her chair.

"What … ah … they are in good health. And the Collinses?"

"I believe they are in good health as well."

He leaned back and glanced around the room, hoping for something to inspire conversation, all the while keeping her in view, drinking in her presence.

She sighed a little uneasily. That was bad enough, but the forced smile she wore, so different from her true smile, almost made her look like another woman. "How very suddenly you all quitted Netherfield last November, Mr. Darcy! It must have been a most agreeable surprise to Mr. Bingley to see you all after him so soon, for, if I recollect right, he went but the day before you left. He and his sisters were well, I hope, when you left London?"

"Perfectly so—I thank you." What game was his muse playing with him now? He had already atoned for that particular deviation from the truth, had he not?

"I have understood that Mr. Bingley has not much idea of ever returning to Netherfield again?"

Where would she have got that notion? The only one who had any inkling of Bingley's plans were Miss Bingley and the Hursts. Had Miss Bingley written to Miss Bennet? "I have never heard him say so, but it is probable that he may spend very little of his time there in future. He has many friends, and he is at a time of life when friends and engagements are continually increasing." And not all of his friends thought the company in Hertfordshire was a good thing.

And those friends were in all likelihood completely wrong. He swallowed hard.

"If he means to be but little at Netherfield, it would be better for the neighborhood that he should give up the place entirely, for then we might possibly get a settled family there." She tossed her head softly, just hinting at disdain. "But perhaps Mr. Bingley did not take the house so much for the convenience of the neighborhood as for his own pleasure, and we must expect him to keep or quit it on the same principle."

"I should not be surprised if he were to give it up as soon as any eligible purchase offers." He stared at his hands. Perhaps he should speak to Bingley on the matter.

Miss Elizabeth made no answer, merely looking at him with something vaguely resembling disapproval. What could he do to change that?

Perhaps a different topic was in order. "This seems a very comfortable house. Lady Catherine, I believe, did a great deal to it when Mr. Collins first came to Hunsford."

She rolled her eyes just a bit. "I believe she did—and I am sure she could not have bestowed her kindness on a more grateful object."

"Mr. Collins appears very fortunate in his choice of a wife."

"Yes, indeed. His friends may well rejoice in his having met with one of the very few sensible women who would have accepted him, or have made him happy if they had. My friend has an excellent understanding—though I am not certain that I consider her marrying Mr. Collins as the wisest thing she ever did. She seems perfectly happy, however, and in a prudential light, it is certainly a very good match for her." Just how many emotions could play across a face in a single moment? He counted no less than five: frustration, teasing, resignation, peace, and something that was not entirely happiness but made a strong effort to appear so.

"It must be very agreeable to her to be settled within so easy a distance of her own family and friends." But who really cared what Mrs. Collins thought of the matter? How did Miss Elizabeth regard distance from a woman's family?

"An easy distance, do you call it? It is nearly fifty miles." She laughed, but it was hardly a happy sound.

"And what is fifty miles of good road? Little more than half a day's journey. Yes, I call it a very easy distance."

"I should never have considered the distance as one of the advantages of the match. I should never have said Mrs. Collins was settled near her family."

"It is a proof of your own attachment to Hertfordshire. Anything beyond the very neighborhood of Longbourn, I suppose, would appear far." Pray, let it not be so!

She pressed back into her chair and shook her head subtly. "I do not mean to say that a woman may not be settled too near her family. Far and the near must be relative and depend on many varying circumstances. Where there is fortune to make the expense of travelling unimportant, distance becomes no evil. But that is not the case here. Mr. and Mrs. Collins have a comfortable income, but not such a one as will allow of frequent journeys. I am persuaded my friend would not call herself near her family under less than half the present distance."

Perhaps then, there was a chance! He leaned toward her. "I imagine you cannot have a right to such very strong local attachment. You cannot have been always at Longbourn."

Elizabeth looked surprised. But what did that mean? Had she never been much away from Longbourn, or did she not consider the possibility with pleasure? Perhaps a different question. "Are you pleased with Kent?"

"It is a very fine county, with ample beauties to boast. I have found many of them here in Rosings Park."

"My aunt would be pleased to hear you say so."

"I imagine you are correct. She seems to prefer the country to being in town. Oh, I think I hear Mrs. Collins coming in. Pray excuse me whilst I fetch her here. She would be most sorry to miss your call." She jumped up and hurried out, taking the sunshine and warmth of the room with her.

He felt her disappearance with the same keenness as when she had left Rosings. This would not do, not at all. There was no choice. He would have to return to the parsonage as often as he could. And perhaps make a better plan for keeping in her company. After all, a woman could be settled too near her family; those were her very promising words!

Each day, each visit, only served to strengthen his attachment to the one his muse deemed essential. On those days he did not attend her, he spent hours over his sketchbook crafting studies of her features, her expressions, even attempting to capture her grace in movement. The sketches took form easily and cleanly, flowing from his pencil to paper as though they had been there all along. Finally, joy had returned to his efforts.

Oddly, though, when he sketched, he usually did not include backgrounds unless they were crucial to the study. But for some reason, they stubbornly appeared in each of his latest pieces. They required so little effort that he nearly ignored them until he found himself drawing a bust of Lady Anne Darcy that Father had commissioned shortly after their marriage. Why was he sketching Miss Elizabeth in the Pemberley gallery?

Because she belonged there.

Darcy dropped his pencil and stared at the sketch with burning eyes and racing heart. The notion had been at the edges of his awareness for some time now with no words to precisely define it. But now they were there, plain as paint on canvas. He could no long deny it, no long avoid it.

That was it—the answer he had avoided seeing for far too long.

His muse would not be satisfied without her constant presence. The only way to obtain that was to make her his wife. Some might argue that a mistress would serve the same purpose, but she was not the sort of woman one dealt with in that fashion, nor would his muse tolerate such treatment. The only way he could have her by his side was as a wife, so that was what he would do.

He had to. There was no alternative. It did not

matter that her family was horrid and her connections low. It did not matter that she had no fortune and her accomplishments were modest at best. It did not matter that most of his family would disapprove and might even shun her. He would ignore all those privations; his muse would permit him no rest otherwise.

When would the Collinses next be away from the parsonage?

His groom brought word that he had seen the Collinses walking out from the parsonage and they were not expected back soon. The man would receive an ample reward! Darcy donned a fresh shirt and cravat and hurried out. Miss Elizabeth had not felt well yesterday; that was sufficient reason for a call, was it not? Not that it was his true purpose, but somehow it felt easier to know he did not need to reveal his honest intentions immediately.

He rang the bell, counting the seconds until he was admitted. Could not the maid move faster to take him to her?

At long last, he reached the parlor near the back of the house. It was a cluttered little room, littered with furniture that did not match and odd bric-a-brac that resembled bits dumped from a peddler's sack. But what was an unattractive room to the company and the purpose he had today?

"Good day, Miss Bennet." He bowed but only received a cold glance from her. "Have you recovered from your headache yesterday?"

"After a fashion, I suppose." She did not look at him directly. Was she still feeling poorly?

She plucked the folds of her skirt, pointedly not

looking at him.

He sat down, but that would hardly do. Energy coursed through his limbs, and if he did not expend it, he might lose any hope of coherent speech. So, he jumped to his feet and paced along the longest side of the room in front of the fireplace.

Surely, she must understand his agitation. That had to be why she said nothing; she was allowing him to soothe himself so that he could speak. She was the very soul of consideration; no doubt, she would not desire to prolong his agony.

He whirled on her, words tumbling out beyond all control. "In vain have I struggled. It will not do. My feelings will not be repressed. You must allow me to tell you how ardently I admire and love you."

Her jaw dropped, and she stared at him, her cheeks bright and her eyes filled with fire. Of course, she should be speechless. Men of his standing were rare, and a proposal in such a circumstance, even if she anticipated it, would certainly still be surprising. Perhaps she was worried, as a sensible woman of her status would be, of the inequality of their match.

He stumbled over his words as he assured her how little he cared for his friends', his family's, nay society's abhorrence of such a connection. That even his best judgment was not enough to stand against the violent passion he felt for her. He concluded with representing to her the strength of that attachment which, in spite of all his endeavors, he had found impossible to conquer and expressing his hope that it would now be rewarded by her acceptance of his hand.

Breathless, he awaited word of his fate. No, the proposal did not come out sounding as it should, certainly not like the hero of some romantic novel. But she would understand. Of course, she would. Theirs was a connection beyond words.

The color rose higher into her cheeks, and she drew a deep breath. Surely, his torment would now end.

"In such cases as this, it is, I believe, the established mode to express a sense of obligation for the sentiments avowed, however unequally they may be returned. It is natural that obligation should be felt, and if I could feel gratitude, I would now thank you." Her hand and her voice trembled. "But I cannot—I have never desired your good opinion, and you have certainly bestowed it most unwillingly. I am sorry to have occasioned pain to anyone. It has been most unconsciously done, however, and I hope will be of short duration. The feelings which, you tell me, have long prevented the acknowledgment of your regard, can have little difficulty in overcoming it after this explanation."

Chilled silence followed, echoing more loudly than any sound could.

Darcy clutched the mantel lest his knees fail. Surely, he had not heard those words. She must be teasing him. But when he searched her face for some sign of jest, there was none. Absolutely none.

He forced out words, barely above a whisper, as the room spun around him. "And this is all the reply which I am to have the honor of expecting? I might, perhaps, wish to be informed why, with so little endeavor at civility, I am thus rejected."

Her eyes bulged, and her nostrils flared. "I might as well enquire why, with so evident a design of offending and insulting me, you chose to tell me that you liked me against your will, against your reason, and even against your character? Was not this some excuse for incivility, if I was uncivil?"

He clenched his fist against the weight of her just accusation.

She rose, slowly, dangerously, her voice honed to a finely-edged weapon. "But I have other provocations. You know I have. Had not my own feelings decided against you, had they been indifferent, or had they even been favorable, do you think that any consideration would tempt me to accept the man who has been the means of ruining, perhaps forever, the happiness of a most beloved sister?"

Why had he not listened to that voice when it had warned him against Miss Bingley's subterfuge? Was this to be the price for his selfishness in choosing his own comfort over the interest of his friend?

"I have every reason in the world to think ill of you. No motive can excuse the unjust and ungenerous part you acted there. You dare not, you cannot deny that you have been the principal, if not the only means, of dividing them from each other, of exposing one to the censure of the world for caprice and instability, the other to its derision for disappointed hopes, and involving them both in misery of the acutest kind. Can you deny that you have done it?" Her tightly-balled fists quivered at her sides.

Something about the way she glowered at him triggered the instincts of a bear baited into a fury—rationality was lost. "I have no wish of denying that I did everything in my power to separate my friend from your sister, or that I rejoice in my success. Towards him I have been kinder than towards myself."

He would probably regret those words, but what did it matter now?

"But it is not merely this affair on which my dislike is founded. Long before it had taken place, my opinion of you was decided. Your character was unfolded in the recital which I received many months ago from Mr. Wickham. On this subject, what can you have to say? In what imaginary act of friendship can you here defend yourself?" It must be righteous indignation that strengthened her stance and edged her voice. She was terrible and magnificent in her fury.

He pulled back his shoulders and stood a little straighter. Somehow this, an unjust accusation, was easier to tolerate. "You take an eager interest in that gentleman's concerns."

"Who that knows what his misfortunes have been can help feeling an interest in him?"

"His misfortunes!" He threw up an open hand. "Yes, his misfortunes have been great indeed."

"And of your infliction. You have reduced him to his present state of poverty. You have withheld the advantages which you must know to have been designed for him. You have deprived the best years of his life, of that independence which was no less his due than his dessert. You have done all this, and yet you can treat the mention of his misfortunes with contempt and ridicule!"

"And this," he crossed the room with quick short steps, "is your opinion of me! This is the estimation in which you hold me! I thank you for explaining it so fully. My faults, according to this calculation, are heavy indeed! But perhaps these offenses might have been overlooked had not your pride been hurt by my honest confession of the scruples that had long prevented my forming any serious design. These bitter accusations might have been suppressed had I with greater policy concealed my struggles and flattered you into the belief of my being impelled by unqualified, unalloyed inclination—by reason, by reflection, by everything. But disguise of every sort is my abhorrence. Nor am I ashamed of the feelings I related. They were natural and just. Could you expect me to rejoice in the inferiority of your connections? To congratulate myself on the hope of relations whose condition in life is so decidedly beneath my own?" The words tumbled forth with venom equal to her own.

Her features turned to ice: glittering, pristine, and sharp. "You are mistaken, Mr. Darcy, if you suppose that the mode of your declaration affected me in any other way than as it spared me the concern which I might have felt in refusing you, had you behaved in a more gentleman-like manner. You could not have made me the offer of your hand in any possible way that would have tempted me to accept it."

The frost wind that carried her words tore the heat from his body and the air from his lungs. *A more gentleman-like manner...* The way those words reverberated through his being, he might never cease hearing them.

"From the very beginning, from the first moment of my acquaintance with you, your manners, impressing me with the fullest belief of your arrogance, your conceit, and your selfish disdain of the feelings of others, were such as to form that ground-work of disapprobation on which succeeding events have built so immoveable a dislike. I had not known you a month before I felt that you were the last man in the world whom I could ever be prevailed on to marry."

The last man … the last man …

He silenced her with an upraised palm. "You have said quite enough, madam. I perfectly comprehend your feelings and have now only to be ashamed of what my own have been. Forgive me for having taken up so much of your time, and accept my best wishes for your health and happiness." He stormed from the room and from the parsonage.

How was it possible that his muse should have directed him so, to convince him of the one thing he needed like air, only to tear it away from him in one awful, dreadful, life-rending moment?

What did she think of him?

In truth some of it was just. He was ill-mannered and ill-spoken, even if truthful, in all his declarations to her. It sounded nothing like a marriage proposal should. But it had been honest and from the heart—was that not enough?

His gut twisted hard as it always did when he tried to run from truth.

No. No, it was not. Not in light of the way he had treated Bingley and his affections. If he dismissed his friend's affections, did he deserve to have the fulfillment of his own? Of course not.

But her accusations extended farther than Bingley. In all her considerations toward Wickham, she was in error, completely and totally. At least in that matter he could acquit himself.

Should he, though? It would hardly change her feelings toward him.

But that was not the point. If she had to dislike him—and nothing would ever change that—at least he could make certain it was for true faults of his own, not cleverly crafted lies.

He stood in the middle of the road and exhaled a ragged breath. With it went all energy, all strength, all hope. Resignation filled the empty places, numb and cold.

The sensation was not unfamiliar. It had held him together through the death of his mother, his father, and through Georgiana's near compromise. It would hold him together now which was the best that he might hope for.

He trudged back to Rosings Park. He had a letter to write.

The next morning Darcy dragged himself out to the walk he knew Miss Elizabeth favored. No amount of sunshine or fair wind could add color to the grey bleakness that surrounded him. An hour and she did not appear. She must be somewhere. Surely, she would not keep to the parsonage when he desperately needed to encounter her in the woods.

Where else might she go? The gates overlooking the park were pleasant this time of day. There was absolutely no reason he should go there, but he did. Naturally, she was not there, so he stalked the grove, striving to walk away the anxious energy that plucked at every nerve.

Wait, could it be? No, surely his muse's dying breaths taunted him with visions that would disappear. Yet it lingered and drew closer! It was!

He held out the letter that he had spent the better part of the night writing and stepped toward her with all the strength he could muster. "I have been walking in the grove for some time in the hope of meeting you. Will you do me the honor of reading that letter?"

With a slight bow, he turned away and rushed into the cover of the trees, the words he had written echoing in his mind:

Be not alarmed, Madam, on receiving this letter, by the apprehension of it containing any repetition of those sentiments, or renewal of those offers, which were last night so disgusting to you. I write without any intention of paining you, or humbling myself, by dwelling on wishes, which, for the happiness of both, cannot be too soon forgotten, and the effort which the formation and the perusal of this letter must occasion should have been spared, had not my character required it to be written and read. You must, therefore, pardon the freedom with which I demand your attention; your feelings, I know, will bestow it unwillingly, but I demand it of your justice.

His errand complete, he sought out his valet and his driver. They would be away from this dreadful place as soon as arrangements could be made, before the death of his muse made marriage to Anne seem like an appropriate punishment for his transgressions against Miss Elizabeth.

✣ Chapter 4

USUALLY ON THE return journey to Pemberley, he took the opportunity to ride alongside the coach at least several hours a day. Little could compare to experiencing the countryside atop a fine horse. But he could find no such solace this time. The entire distance, some one hundred and eighty miles, was spent shuttered in the coach with the drapes drawn closed.

How could he look out upon a landscape that had turned grey and drab? Even the sunshine lost its warmth, its life-giving essence and the wind all traces of hope. It was all gone.

Behaved in a more gentlemanlike manner … the last man in the world …

When he closed his eyes, he saw nothing. Absolutely nothing, and he probably never would again. Until that fateful interview, when he shut his eyes, images took shape: drawings, paintings, colors, and forms. Boredom had made little sense to him then; neither had loneliness. His muse had always stood sufficient company to stave off both.

But now he was alone. More alone than he had ever been. Without his muse. Without her. Empty. Cold. Sterile.

Surely, he would never create again. How could he hold a brush or crayon or pencil now? The only image he could call upon was that look she had given him when she crushed his fondest dream. Though her justice was incomplete and not all her accusations were true, there was enough righteousness in them that he could not bear to hear them again.

Perhaps it would be better this way. He would miss the ecstasy of the creative impulses, but being free of its torment was no small thing. The relief might be worth the dull dreariness that was his world now.

At least there would be peace. At least after a fashion.

Would it be so bad to live as other men did? They survived it well enough. Certainly, he could learn, too. He had to.

Pemberley, as always, welcomed him with open arms. She was never so happy as when her only son was in residence. Or at least Mrs. Reynolds told him so when he returned. It was difficult to argue with her kindly smile.

He dove into the work of the estate with a fervor that rivaled some of his most creative periods. Perhaps his beloved estate would take the place of his muse, soothing his soul with useful, if mundane, employ.

Fitzwilliam and Georgiana both insisted that he was working too hard. But how could they understand? While Georgiana was indeed proficient on her instrument, she was proficient, not inspired. It was work and effort for her, not the joyous release that it might have been. She did not repine her situation, not knowing her art in any other way. If she had, she would have understood Darcy's aching need to fill the vacancy in his being with busyness.

⁓⁂⁓

As spring melted into summer, the work of the estate lessened, settling into a bland routine that he could manage far too easily. Boredom, with its bleak mendacity that muddled activity with productivity, settled in.

Then the letters began. The dreadful, awful, tempting letters.

The first one came at the beginning of June. Followed by another a fortnight later. Then they arrived weekly. By the final week of July, the missives were coming daily. All droning the same ghastly message.

Aunt Catherine's precise, angular hand reminded him of his duty to his family, the brilliance of the match, the necessity of an heir—all leading to the same horrible conclusion. He must marry Anne.

As her demands became more frantic, more insistent, more guilt-inducing, his better sense began to wear away, tempted to silence the droning voice in his head. In a moment of clear-headedness, or was it desperation? —it was difficult to tell anymore, but whatever it was—he felt the determination to thwart Aunt Catherine more strongly than he had felt anything in months.

How ironic that once he should feel again, the feelings would be more torment. But the relief of renewed sensibilities forbade him from turning his back on it. Instead, he crafted his bastion against Aunt Catherine's plague.

The small room off Pemberley's gallery had been the storage room for most of his works. His ego did not permit him to litter all of Pemberley's walls with art of his own making. The place usually remained locked and off limits to even the servants.

Since he would never paint again, he turned it into a shrine to what might have been. On the walls, he hung the finished canvases revealing his study of the nymph whose face was Miss Elizabeth's. On easels and stands rested the unfinished pieces and sketches that would now remain incomplete, a tribute to the price a vengeful muse might exact. Yes, it was a painful place, to be sure, but it was a place in which he could feel again. And those sensations would provide him a sure guard against a moment of weakness that might trap him in Aunt Catherine's web.

At the beginning of August, a different sort of letter arrived. Bingley invited him to meet him and his sisters in Derby to enjoy the theater there. From there, with Darcy's permission of course, the party might return with Darcy to Pemberley to enjoy a summer house party there.

Darcy was on the verge of refusing when yet another missive arrived from Aunt Catherine. A little time away from her constant missives could hardly be a bad thing. Moreover, Georgiana's spirits seemed a bit low, and this sort of diversion would do her well. So, they went off with instructions to Mrs. Reynolds that they would return in a week.

Although Bingley's company and all the activity that accompanied him were distracting, mere distraction was not enough. Bingley's presence, even here away from Hertfordshire, served to remind him too much of her. A day before the week was complete, he had to leave, excusing himself with the promise that he was ensuring Pemberley would be ready to receive them when they arrived.

Yes, it was a lie, but surely it was a harmless one. Far less damaging than explaining that he could no longer tolerate company. Even Bingley's equanimity could not withstand such honesty.

The weather proved fine and his horse in high spirits, so the ride back was pleasant and even a mite engaging. Wait. Was that the river that ran the length of Pemberley? Why had he chosen that route? When had he chosen that route? How had he become so distracted? How long had it been since that had happened, and why was it happening now?

Uneasiness—or was it anticipation? —with all the requisite sensations coursed through his limbs. Bah! He could not ride in such a state.

He delivered his horse to the stable and continued on foot. What instructions did Mrs. Reynolds need to prepare for Bingley's party tomorrow? Pray the party did not expect him to host good dinners and large parties on their behalf. Bingley certainly would not, but his sisters? They just might.

Perhaps it would be wise to craft an appropriate response just in case. He rubbed his fist along his stubbled chin.

"Mr. Darcy!"

Their eyes met.

He staggered back as though he had run headlong into a wall. She blushed.

It was her. It was Miss Elizabeth.

Here. At Pemberley.

His mouth went dry and wooly; his feet rooted in place, his lungs barely responded to his command to breathe.

She pressed her hand to her chest, eyes darting to look anywhere but at him. "Pray excuse me, sir. The housekeeper said that you were away from the house and would not return from some time."

"I have returned a day earlier than anticipated."

Her jaw hung agape as though at a loss for what to say.

"Are your family well?" Not an original question but they were words, and he could say them; that was miracle enough.

"Yes, they are, thank you." Perhaps it was just in her surprise that she had forgotten her earlier feelings toward him, but her voice held no disdain. He probably should not hope.

"And how do you find Pemberley? Is it to your liking?" He stared at her face, willing himself to listen as he never had before.

"I can hardly think anyone upon visiting it could find fault with it." Her voice held the promise of a smile.

Was it possible? How could that be?

"I am pleased to hear it. Your good opinion is well worth the earning. Would you introduce me to your party?" He gestured to the man and woman who stood just behind her, beneath the shade of his favorite tree.

"Of course." She beckoned them near. "May I present the Gardiners, my aunt and uncle from Gracechurch Street." She emphasized the last words, asking a question that dare not be spoken.

"I am delighted to make your acquaintance." He bowed and beckoned to the gardener who had been standing in the shadows, watching the entire affair. "Pray take them around the grounds and show them the best views. You will excuse me." He bowed again and strode away.

Truly, he did not want to leave, but he had to. If he had any hope of ever breathing or thinking again, he had to.

What was she doing here? He was never to see her again. Was that not what his muse had insisted? Yes, that is how it had been.

Her laugh rang through the trees some distance behind him.

At least, he though it had. But she was here! He stared into the sky. His knees threatened to melt beneath him. Had the color just returned to the world? It had—that wonderous shade of blue had not been there earlier.

One did not waste such an opportunity! He had to show her—for he certainly could not say the words—how desperately he longed for redemption. The quest could not wait a moment longer.

Where would the gardener have taken them? Blast it all! He should never have left them. Of course, the woods near the river: his favorite spot for fishing. That had to be it. He broke into a run.

Yes, there they were. He could just make them out at the bridge near the coppiced woods. He slowed to a brisk walk; it would not do to run at them. How easily that could be misconstrued. Besides, he needed just a moment to capture the image in his mind, just in case his muse permitted him to commit it to paper: the dappled sunlight across the bridge framed her against the river's sparkling currents.

"Miss Bennet," he stopped near her and bowed. Hopefully she would not detect him still panting. "I pray you will forgive my prior departure. That business is now complete, though. Might I join your party on your walk?"

She stammered a bit, high color in her cheeks, but eventually managed to express an affirmative. He might have apologized for interrupting and excused himself had not a pretty smile accompanied her words.

Mr. Gardiner trundled over and immediately took over the conversation. Well-dressed and with a confident bearing, he was certainly a relation for whom Miss Elizabeth need not blush. How quickly men of good sense and breeding made themselves known. His position in trade notwithstanding, he was both.

From the corner of his eye, Darcy could just make out a dimple in Miss Elizabeth's cheek. Perhaps, with a very little effort, he could encourage that expression.

"Do you care for fishing, sir?"

Mr. Gardiner stood a little straighter, his eyes twinkling much like Miss Elizabeth's did when pleased. "I do indeed, sir, when I have the opportunity, of course. With most of our time spent in London, I fear I do not often have the chance."

"You must take it whilst you are here, then. I insist. I imagine you have not brought tackle of your own, so you must use some of mine. I will have it no other way."

Mrs. Gardiner approached Miss Elizabeth and looped her arm in her niece's. She whispered something in Miss Elizabeth's ear.

"I cannot say. I am all astonishment," Miss Elizabeth whispered back.

Astonishment? That was probably a good thing, all told.

"Mr. Gardiner," Mrs. Gardiner released Elizabeth and approached her husband, "pray forgive me for interrupting, but I am much fatigued, and poor Elizabeth's arm is inadequate for my support. Would you take me?" She extended her hand toward him.

"You will excuse me, sir?" He dipped his head and tucked his wife's hand in the crook of his arm to walk slightly ahead of Darcy.

Yes, it seemed far too convenient and a little conspiratorial. Had it been anyone else, he would have excused himself back to the house with the sensation of a rat avoiding a trap. But this was entirely different. The Gardiners were rapidly becoming his favorite among the many Bennet relations with whom he was already acquainted.

Darcy dropped back a bit to walk beside Miss Elizabeth. "A party will join me early tomorrow, and among them are some who will claim an acquaintance with you—Mr. Bingley and his sisters."

She stiffened a mite but did not comment further.

"There is also one other person in the party who more particularly wishes to be known to you. Will you allow me, or do I ask too much, to introduce my sister to your acquaintance during your stay at Lambton?"

She looked up at him, scanning his face. Was she—yes, it seemed she understood all he implied but did not say. "I would be very pleased to make her acquaintance."

She was pleased by something he had done! Pleased!

His heart thundered, resounding in his ears, as heat surged through his veins. Had he been warm at all since that day in Kent? Quite possibly not—and he would relish it for every moment he had.

They arrived at the Gardiners' carriage far too soon. But he was permitted to hand the ladies into the carriage. She had permitted his touch!

His head swam with the possibility—perhaps he had been forgiven, or at least offered a second chance by a muse convinced of his repentance.

And he would not fail.

He could not.

No sooner did the Gardiners' carriage disappear down the road, but Darcy dashed into his storage room turned shrine—his attic studio had already been emptied into that room. Raw, unfettered energy surged through every bone, every nerve, every tendon. Like a fire lit by lightning, it flared and spread into the entirety of his being. Who knew how long it might last? It could be a very fleeting thing—the last opportunity he might have to put brush to canvas. Only a fool would waste time eating or sleeping at such a moment.

And such a moment it was. In the candlelight, the essence of his muse blossomed on the canvas in its purest, truest form—her eyes and her lips as she smiled on him, genuinely smiled upon him—an expression he had never been blessed with before. As dawn rose, streaming rosy light through the windows, he had not finished, but the piece was complete enough that no matter what happened, he could finish it. He would finish it. The crowning glory on this singular study demanded by his muse.

He set his brush aside, sank into a chair, and slept, slumped against the windowsill.

A few hours later, he roused with the sounds of visitors arriving. Bingley—in the morning? How unheard of! And how perfect. With a small amount of effort, he could prevail upon Bingley to pay a call, and they could be off to call upon the inn before midday! He ran upstairs for fresh clothes.

Bingley received the idea with all the vigor with which he received most suggestions of diversion, perhaps just a mite more. Soon, he, Bingley, and Georgiana were bundled into Darcy's carriage on the way to Lambton.

<hr />

Georgiana and Bingley chatted as they drove. How did they find so much to talk about? Thankfully, they allowed Darcy quiet space for his thoughts. He could not have conversed with them even if he wanted to.

So much depended on this exchange of civilities. It had to go well; it had to be right. What would he say to her? How would he introduce his friend and his sister? Was there any way he could pour his heart into those few words in such a way that she might truly understand?

As they approached the inn, a face—hers, it had to be—appeared in the window. Perhaps it was simply his imagination, but it seemed she was watching for their arrival. It was hard to frame that possibility as anything but a good omen. Still, his heart beat faster, and his throat constricted as he handed Georgiana down from the carriage. A serving girl led them up a dark, squeaky staircase to the Gardiners' rented chambers, the best the inn had to offer.

Mr. and Mrs. Gardiner greeted them graciously, but it was Miss Elizabeth's reaction that most interested him. He introduced Bingley and Georgiana, utterly forgetting anything he had planned to say. Still, she received them with all the warmth of a welcomed acquaintance.

Miss Elizabeth seemed to take particular interest in Georgiana. Though the urge to protect his still vulnerable sister rose up, something held him back. Perhaps it was the soft light in Miss Elizabeth's eyes or the delicacy of her voice. But it was clear: Miss Elizabeth would be as gentle and tender as Georgiana deserved.

Of course, she would. Would his muse have selected a less worthy woman?

Bingley quickly commanded the conversation, as he usually did, making enquiries after the health and happiness of her family and asking in a more general fashion after the news in Hertfordshire. It seemed he was hoping for some specific piece of information but was not yet willing to ask.

Though he listened carefully, Darcy could detect no note of anger or bitterness in her responses.

But the barest crease in Miss Elizabeth's brow suggested a touch of lingering sadness, no doubt in regard to her sister's disappointment. He could not fault her for that feeling; in fact, it was to her credit that she might feel so deeply for Miss Bennet.

Remarkably, he caught her stealing glances at him. It was difficult to discern at first, but no, she was watching him—but why? Her face betrayed no trace of the animosity he had seen at Hunsford. But what was she thinking behind her mild expression? Her mind was far too lively to be as quiescent as her demeanor.

At one point their gazes met, and instead of turning away, embarrassed, she offered him the teasing, tantalizing hint of a smile.

Was it possible? Could it be true? By some unearned miracle, had she changed her opinion of him? It seemed too much to hope that his letter could have made that material a difference in her perceptions of him. But if it did, he would not question his good fortune. Unfortunately, the tantalizing possibility rendered him mute and unable to ferret out any further information.

A quarter of an hour passed, and neither Bingley nor Georgiana had shown any sign of being ready to depart. So, too, did the Gardiners appear to take pleasure in the company. What else could he do but content himself to remain far longer than a call should linger.

Perhaps that was a mistake, not for the sake of his company, but for himself. After half an hour in her company, he was loath to depart. How could he leave when she had smiled upon him?

Bingley, in his usual haphazard fashion, offered the remedy without even knowing. He made a light-hearted remark about Pemberley's excellent victuals. Georgiana glanced back at Darcy. Of course, they must be invited to dinner!

In mere moments, the invitation expanded from just the evening to all of the next day. He bade Mr. Gardiner come to fish and the ladies even hinted that they might call upon Georgiana in the morning. A whole day with her at Pemberley? It was too great a boon to comprehend.

The enthusiastic acceptance of the invitations soothed the bitterness of their departure, at least enough that he could pass the remainder of the day in tolerably good spirits. Bingley deserved as much for the immeasurable service he had just rendered.

The next morning, near dawn, Darcy made his way to his shrine. There was something about the light of dawn as it crept across his paintings. He wanted, he needed to see his paintings of her in that light. Perhaps it was that light that would assure him he had done justice to her. Perhaps it was just his fickle muse. Either way, he would not resist.

His muse welcomed him into that space with a golden glow that he could almost hear, bidding him join her. Could a voice sound like sunlight?

His most recent creation, silhouetted by a dawn-filled window, called to him. His spine tingled, and he reminded himself to take a breath. That look in her eye from yesterday as she had regarded him with favor—and could it be, possibly some affection—was captured perfectly.

What sort of sign was this—that she would be there with him and never leave, or that now her image was committed to canvas, she would leave him forever? Either could be true.

Surely his muse could not be so cruel as to take her from him forever. Surely not! Whatever it took to make certain she would remain with him, he would do it.

No matter what.

The sunshine voice said something that he could not quite discern. The tone was not angry but perhaps stern? A warning, perhaps? As long as his muse was not angry with him, it was enough.

At the earliest moment that their arrival would be considered polite, the Gardiners' coach made its way up the road to Pemberley Manor. They were welcomed in, and the ladies were shown to the parlor to sit with Georgiana, her companion, and the Bingley sisters.

The gentlemen excused themselves to enjoy some sport fishing at the river. Would that he could have excused himself from that pleasure to sit with the ladies, but that would be far too irregular. Better to show himself disciplined and be a respectable host to the gentlemen. Certainly, Miss Elizabeth and his muse would approve.

Naturally, the gentlemen enjoyed the enterprise for several very long hours. Excruciatingly long hours. Thankfully, Bingley was there to make small talk and entertain the men with Darcy's participation only required for commentary about Pemberley, its grounds and buildings. He was just the sort of friend Darcy needed: the sort who could make him look hospitable and generous even when he was not feeling it.

When the gentlemen tired of their sport—truly, how could they have dragged it out so long in the first place? —they returned to the house to share refreshments with the ladies in the drawing room.

Darcy lingered back a few moments. Miss Elizabeth often left him so tongue-tied that it might be wise to take a few moments to prepare a few intelligent sentences of conversation in case he was so called upon.

"Pray, Miss Eliza, are not the Derbyshire militia removed from Meryton? They must be a great loss to your family." That was Miss Bingley's voice.

Darcy gasped. The dreadful, conniving creature. He had recently begun to question her character; this was proof she was worse than he thought. If he suspected she knew about the goings-on at Ramsgate, he would march into the room and throw her out directly. But she could not, so he would tolerate her presence a little longer.

"I cannot imagine why you would suggest such a thing, Miss Bingley. What would give you to think so?" That was Mrs. Gardiner. Calm, level, and direct. No wonder Miss Elizabeth esteemed her so. What an excellent woman she was, the kind Georgiana needed to know.

A few moments later, Miss Elizabeth ducked out of the drawing room. Where was she going? Had Miss Bingley's remark distressed her that much?

Of course, it had.

Darcy followed at a discreet distance. She might not desire company, but he had to make certain she was well.

She walked briskly toward the gallery. Mrs. Reynolds must have taken them there when they toured Pemberley. It must be a good sign that she would turn to his favorite room in the moment of her distress.

He peeked through the gallery door. No! Heavens no! He had left the door to his private room open! She headed directly toward it as if drawn there by a force beyond herself.

She stepped inside and gasped. The sound—not anguish, not joy, but what was it? —reverberated through the gallery and through his soul.

He ran for the room, almost colliding with her just inside the door. The morning sun embraced her, invited her farther in as though she belonged here. And it was true; she did—his muse had declared it so.

She ignored him and moved among the paintings in an atmosphere heavy with the nutty fragrance of drying linseed oil, staring at each one, saying nothing. Every muscle clenched, rooting him in place, lest he disturb her reverie. Each lift of her brow, tilt of her head, widening of her eyes, all spoke more than mere words alone could convey. At long last, she reached his newest work, leaning close to peer at the still-wet brush strokes.

Finally, she turned to him, eyes wide. "I do not understand."

He threw his head back, laced his hands behind his head, and stared at the ceiling. "What can I say?"

"So many? Why?"

"I do not know how to explain."

"Surely, there must be a reason." She stepped a little closer.

"There is often no reason why one's muse demands what it does."

"A muse?"

Did she have to ask such a thing? No one had ever dared ask him to explain. But no, she had a right. If anyone should know, it was she. He could not meet her gaze, though. "A spirit, an inspiration, a demanding mistress who insists an artist obey her commands lest she abandon him to a world weathered and colorless."

She wandered back to his first painting of the nymph. "Tell me about this one."

He followed her and stood just behind her shoulder. "We had just arrived in Hertfordshire. I had not been able to paint in months. I was near Bedlam. Then we went to the assembly, and I saw you there. That night, my muse returned to me and insisted I paint. This was the form that took shape."

"You cannot see the nymph's face."

"Bingley said the same thing to me—and it tormented me until I understood. It was because I did not know you then. You see her face becoming clearer in the later pieces of the study." He beckoned her toward those.

Miss Elizabeth stopped at each, hand clasped behind her back, studying it, not with a critical eye, but one that seemed fascinated—dare he even say she seemed drawn to what she saw?

"She is lovely." A lovely rosy pink spread across her cheeks.

"I am pleased she meets your approval. I covet your good opinion." Pray she would grant it!

"I still do not understand."

How could she not? "I have explained it all to you."

Her brow knit tight, and she chewed her lower lip, her head shaking slowly. "You have? I do not recall ever speaking about your paintings."

"We did not. But I did tell you nonetheless."

"Pray forgive me, I must ask, when?" Her wide eyes suggested she truly wanted to know.

He swallowed hard, barely able to force his trembling voice to whisper. "In vain have I struggled. It will not do. My feelings will not be repressed. You must allow me to tell you how ardently I admire and love you."

She gasped and pressed a hand to her chest.

"I meant that then, and I am afraid I mean it now as well."

Oh, the look she gave him. Astonishment. Relief? Yes, it seemed so. And—dare he believe it—joy? Oh, pray that was indeed what he saw—

Mrs. Reynold's rapid knock echoed off the door. "Pray forgive me, sir!"

It was difficult not to growl at her. Treating the servants civilly, especially one as valued as Mrs. Reynolds, was not just wise, it was right. Still though, could she have contrived to appear at a worse possible moment?

"A servant just came from the inn with letters for the young lady. He said she had mentioned she had been anticipating them and thought they might be urgent." Mrs. Reynolds held up a silver salver with several folded missives.

The inn's servant thought there might be some reward in it for his efforts, no doubt. "Give him a coin for his troubles."

She passed the letters to Miss Elizabeth and beat a hasty retreat.

He forced himself to keep an appropriate distance. It would not do to appear to want to read over her shoulder. "Is there some concern from Hertfordshire? Are you anticipating some news of import?"

She shrugged, her brows flashing up just a bit. "It is not like Jane to delay in writing. I have been concerned, but there is no more specific worry than that."

"Pray, take a moment to read over your letters and ease your mind. Our conversation can, it should, wait for your mind to be at ease." Moreover, it would give him a few moments to compose a proper renewal of his offer just in case it was wanted.

If only he would be so favored!

She was right. His first attempt had been contemptable—utterly and completely. Though he had not planned on renewing his addresses today, failing to seize upon the opportunity now would be criminal. If he tried, he must ensure it was properly done.

She glanced from the letters, to him, and back again. "I believe you are right. Thank you for your understanding."

He brought a stool to her and retreated to the window to give her a measure of privacy.

She tittered under her breath and murmured. "This one was misdirected—no wonder, for Jane wrote the direction very ill indeed."

Excellent! That should set her mind at ease—a much better state for her to receive him in. It had been a mistake to look at her, though. He could not tear his eyes away. Was it really invading her privacy if he watched her as she read? It was hardly as though he could detect the content of the letter from his vantage point.

No angry warning jabbed at him. Surely, it would be all right.

The gentle glow in her eyes must be for her sister. Such a kind and affectionate heart she had. Would she one day hold the same sentiments toward Georgiana? Was it too much to hope that she would? There was no more deserving recipient than she, and, no doubt, Miss Elizabeth would be unfailingly kind toward her regarding her troubles with—that man. And perhaps, just perhaps, Georgiana might be a good sort of sister to Miss Elizabeth as well. Surely, she would not repine a younger sister who was not silly and romping.

No! Something was wrong, very wrong. Her hand trembled, and she did not breathe. Her eyes were wide, shining with tears. What had happened?

She tore the second letter open; tiny gasps for breath escaping as she did. Her hands shook so hard she nearly dropped the pages. How could he not go to her to comfort her? But how could he invade when he had not been invited?

He held his breath along with her, tense and ready to spring.

Tears trickled down her cheek, and he was at her side—to do what, he did not know, but he had to be there.

"Oh! Where, where is my uncle?" She sprang from her seat and ran into him.

He caught her upper arms to steady her from falling. How pale and fragile she seemed.

"I beg your pardon, but I must leave you. I must find Mr. Gardiner this moment, on business that cannot be delayed; I have not a moment to lose." She struggled to see the door around him.

"Good God! what is the matter?" No, that was neither polite nor gentlemanly, but it was all he could say in the moment. He collected himself with a deep breath. "I will not detain you a minute, but let me, or let the servant, go after Mr. and Mrs. Gardiner. You are not well enough; you cannot go yourself. Not yet, you need a moment." And she needed to tell him what was wrong.

She trembled in his grasp and slowly sank back on to the stool.

Had he ever seen one so bereft, so alone? "Let me call a maid or Mrs. Reynolds. Is there nothing you could take to give you present relief? A glass of wine, shall I get you one? You are greatly distressed." There had to be some way to help!

"No, I thank you." She dabbed her eyes with her sleeve. "There is nothing the matter with me. I am quite well. I am only distressed by some dreadful news which I have just received from Longbourn." She burst into tears and for a few minutes could not speak another word.

Darcy hovered over her, pressing his handkerchief into the dainty hands. Oh, the impotence of not knowing her distress! Had her mother taken ill, or perhaps died? Worse still, it could be her father. Longbourn would then go to Collins who would no doubt throw them out immediately.

But with that he could help. If she accepted his offer, then he would see her mother and sisters well settled. Perhaps though, he should not offer marriage now; he should settle them all first, then she would understand his good will. Perhaps then she might accept him. Yes, that would be better.

She sniffled and swallowed hard. He held his jaws clamped shut. Pray she would simply speak!

"I have just had a letter from Jane with such dreadful news. It cannot be concealed from any one. My youngest sister has left all her friends—has eloped. She has thrown herself into the power of—of Mr. Wickham. They are gone off together from Brighton. You know him too well to doubt the rest. She has no money, no connections, nothing that can tempt him to—she is lost forever." She covered her face with her hands and huddled into her lap, rocking just a bit.

The blood drained from his face, and his joints went rigid. Wickham. Wickham! But why—Miss Elizabeth was right—her sister had nothing that would tempt Wickham…

… except revenge against Darcy.

How had he identified Darcy's muse's fixation upon Miss Elizabeth? It should be no surprise that he did—it had happened before. Wickham had used that discovery during university to tease and vex him with small distractions, but then left that tack to pursue something bigger as he set his sights on Georgiana's dowry. Surely, his actions now were revenge for those thwarted plans.

"When I consider—" how thin and frail her voice, "—that I might have prevented it! I who knew what he was. Had I but explained some part of it only—some part of what I learnt—to my own family! Had his character been known, this could not have happened. But it is all, all too late now."

"I am grieved, indeed. Grieved—shocked. But is it certain, absolutely certain?" If only he could snatch those letters and read them for himself!

"Oh yes! They left Brighton together on Sunday night and were traced almost to London, but not beyond; they are certainly not gone to Scotland."

"And what has been done, what has been attempted, to recover her?" Pray her father was not so lost as to abandon her entirely.

"My father is gone to London, and Jane has written to beg my uncle's immediate assistance, and we shall be off, I hope, in half an hour." She sobbed into her hands, muttering, "But nothing can be done. I know very well that nothing can be done. How is such a man to be worked on? How are they even to be discovered? I have not the smallest hope. It is every way horrible!"

If only he could take her into his arms to comfort her and promise that all would be well. It had to be. He would make it so.

"You gave me the power to have done something. When my eyes were opened to his real character. Oh, had I known what I ought, what I dared, to do! But I knew not—I was afraid of doing too much. Wretched, wretched, mistake!"

Had she kept his secrets to protect Georgiana? What other motive might she have had? And if she had, her current misery was also his fault.

Darcy paced the length of the room and back lest his rage be unleashed, and she misunderstand its object. Was it not enough for Wickham to have tried to take his sister? Had he not learned from that endeavor? The unmitigated gall that he should now attempt to steal from Darcy again. It would not work; no, it would not.

Mrs. Gardiner's concerned face peeked through the doorway, Mrs. Reynolds just behind her. Miss Elizabeth would be in far better hands with her aunt. At least now, though, he knew what he should do. "I am afraid you have been long desiring my absence, nor have I anything to plead in excuse of my stay, but real, though unavailing, concern. Would to heaven that anything could be either said or done on my part, that might offer consolation to such distress! But I will not torment you with vain wishes which may seem purposely to ask for your thanks. This unfortunate affair will, I fear, prevent my sister's having the pleasure of dining with you at Pemberley today."

"Oh, yes. Be so kind as to apologize for us to Miss Darcy. Say that urgent business calls us home immediately. Conceal the unhappy truth as long as it is possible. I know it cannot be long." She peeked up over her hands. How like her to recognize Georgiana's delicate feelings at such a time as this. Her tear-stained face wrenched fierce determination from his soul.

If there were anything that could more secure his resolve in this moment, he could not imagine its form. He offered her a slight bow and approached Mrs. Gardiner. "Pray, madam, ask Mrs. Reynolds for anything that Pemberley might offer to assist you in this time. You shall have it. I insist."

She murmured something that was half-gratitude and half-confusion and rushed to Miss Elizabeth's side. If only he could take charge of the situation, offer assurances and consolation in the face of the news Mrs. Gardiner would soon hear. But that was not his place.

Not yet.

He strode out, brisk and purposeful. First, he must tell his valet to pack to leave in the morning. Next, there were letters to be written and posted today. His steward needed to be made aware of his travel plans, and Mrs. Reynolds needed instruction regarding the same. Surely all that could be accomplished yet today. He would leave at first light, no matter what.

❧ Chapter 5

HE HAD BEEN told the Gardiners had left directly for Hertfordshire that very afternoon. It was only to be expected. Still though, the news cut like a knife.

Mrs. Reynolds had packed a hamper for the Gardiners and Miss Elizabeth to ease the discomforts of hunger and thirst along their journey. Not that Miss Elizabeth would likely be interested in such base things as food and drink in the midst of her distress. Still it was a token, hopefully to remind her that she had friends willing to exercise efforts on her behalf.

Bingley had been most concerned about Darcy's rapid departure so soon after the house party's arrival, but he assured Bingley the urgent business could not wait. The house party could and should continue without him. It would be good for Georgiana to practice being a hostess to them.

Perhaps he should have told Bingley the entire truth, but that would doubtless have ended in an uncomfortable revelation of the part he had played in separating Bingley from Miss Bennet. Yes, he would have to confess everything soon enough, but not while there was an urgent matter demanding his intervention.

He would find Wickham and make him pay for what he had done. He would make things right for Miss Elizabeth, and he would marry her. All those were certain.

And maddeningly uncertain at the same time.

His generous muse had brought Miss Elizabeth to him but now demanded that he prove himself worthy of the gift. And he would do that. Somehow, he would.

But now he had to determine how.

If Wickham and Lydia were indeed in London and not gone off to Scotland, that was far better news than Miss Elizabeth realized. Darcy had connections in London, and he knew Wickham's connections there. No doubt Wickham's associates were sworn to secrecy, but the kind of people that allied with Wickham were also the sort that could be bought … and bought rather easily. That was in his favor.

And he knew exactly where to begin: Mrs. Younge. The despicable woman had taken a house in Edward Street and rented rooms to lodgers. Where else would Wickham begin but in a place that might offer him succor that he might not have to repay?

<hr />

If anything, Mrs. Younge proved herself more canny and conniving than she had been when she had offered Georgiana to Wickham, like a lamb to the wolf. Three times he had to return with increasing promises of blunt and favors before she gave Wickham up. No doubt she thought herself driving a hard bargain, but in truth, the intelligence was cheaply won and worth every penny and more. How disappointed she would be to learn just how much Darcy had been willing to pay.

According to her, Wickham and Lydia were hidden away in cheap lodgings just a few streets away, in a part of town Darcy hoped Georgiana and Miss Elizabeth would never see. To there he made haste the next morning. With any luck, he would have Lydia's situation negotiated by midday and take the good news to Miss Elizabeth by evening.

Who was he fooling? Himself alone, most likely. Nothing should ever be so easy. No errand demanded by his muse could be unfraught with hardship and strain. But whatever it took, he would show himself worthy.

A frumpy woman with stringy grey hair that framed her plump face—perhaps the housekeeper, perhaps the purveyor of the lodgings, let him in and pointed to the stairs. "Third room on the right," she wheezed.

No sunlight actually reached the windows of the third-rate townhouse, leaving the interior dark and dank. The entire place smelt of gin, sweat, and debauchery. How welcome Wickham must feel.

Darcy marched up the stairs and pounded on the door.

The moment he laid eyes on Wickham, he nearly lost control. He had been taught too well to sink so low as to physically engage Wickham, but a tongue lashing was an entirely different matter.

"Darcy! How good of you to call upon me. I had no idea of you being in town." Wickham ushered him inside. He wore no jacket, his cravat draped, untied, across his shoulders. His wrinkled shirt hung open at the neck as did his red waistcoat, unbuttoned across his chest. How could he receive anyone in such a state of undress?

The room was cluttered with tattered furniture and swathed in dust. The odor of stale food and gin hung in the air, probably a permanent fixture of the lodgings.

"Naturally. If you had known I was here, you would have hidden yourself more carefully." Darcy picked his way across the floor littered with garments and other personal debris.

Wickham pointed him toward a chair covered with a filthy shirt. Darcy stood behind it.

"Is that any way to greet your old friend?" Wickham draped himself across a shabby, faded wingback.

"Our days of friendship are long since gone."

"Then why have you come, except to renew our excellent acquaintance?" That smile, that laugh! Both needed to be erased from Wickham's face as soon as possible.

"I seek an audience with Miss Lydia Bennet."

"Whatever for?" Wickham snorted.

"She has quit the protection of her friends and family and has entered under yours. I wish to ensure her safe and whole." Darcy balled his fists behind his back.

"She is no prisoner of mine. She is here of her own will. Talk to her all you wish; you will find no different." He called over his shoulder, "Lydia! Lydia, do come out and meet our guest."

Lydia burst forth from a shadowed doorway, wrapped in a sloppy dressing gown. One could only imagine what was—or was not—underneath. Darcy could make out the lines of a rumpled bed in the background. Pray that they were betrothed, and this might be at least a modicum less distasteful.

"Mr. Darcy would very much like to talk to you." He winked at her.

Lydia pranced barefoot to Wickham's side. "La! What has he to do with me?"

"Apparently, he is concerned for your welfare." He slipped his arm around her waist.

"I do not see why. But as you can see, I am entirely well and quite happy, I might add." She leaned down close to Wickham.

"You do not have to remain in this situation."

"Why ever would I want to quit it?"

"These accommodations," Darcy sniffed—he could not help it, much as he tried, "are hardly the style to which you are accustomed."

"I think little of that! The company alone is sufficient to make any privation irrelevant." She batted her eyes at Wickham who flashed his brows at Darcy.

Just how much gin had he plied the girl with to make her lose all her sense?

"You do not need to stay, you know. I would be happy to assist you in returning to your friends." He would also be happy to toss her over his shoulder and abscond with her to the Gardiners' doorstep.

"I have no desire to return." She dropped into Wickham's lap and looped her arms around his neck.

"But your situation is … disgraceful! Your reputation is in danger, and the damage to your family and sisters is considerable." No sense in mentioning that her own reputation was not just endangered but irrevocably ruined.

"La! You exaggerate. I cannot imagine where you get such an idea from! Indeed, I cannot. We will be married, and I will return home a married woman." She kissed Wickham's chest and he grinned like a wolf about to feed. "What harm can that bring to my sisters at all? If nothing else, I will be able to offer them introductions and assist them in finding husbands of their own. I will be their benefactor."

"And when exactly shall this wedding be?"

She glanced at Wickham, and they exchanged shrugs. "We have not fixed a date."

"And that does not bother you?" Had her mother taught her nothing?

"We have hardly been in London long enough to fix a date. We have not had time to attend Holy Services yet to present ourselves to the vicar." She leaned into Wickham. "Once that is done, we can begin to consider the wedding."

"I see. Does that not bother you?"

She waved him off. "Of course not. It will all take place in due course, and we will be married when the time is right."

He gripped his hands together and leaned forward. "What, if any, assurances have you that it will take place at all?"

She turned her back on Darcy and looked directly at Wickham. "You are right, my love. Darcy is quite tedious and dull. But do not be afraid, my dear. I have no intentions of leaving your side." She glanced over her shoulder. "I do not imagine there is anything further to be said, Mr. Darcy. I think I shall go for a walk." She jumped up, grabbed a bonnet from the table near the door and flounced out.

"You see, it is just as I told you. She is hardly my prisoner."

"She is drunk and indecent. How can you allow her out of your rooms like that?"

"The housekeeper will not let her out on the streets. She will direct her back to me soon enough."

Darcy dragged his hand down his face. Stubborn and foolish, he might have been able to work on. But stubborn, foolish and plied with drink? There was nothing he could do to affect her. "So then, when will you marry her?"

Wickham laughed. "Marry her? I am in hardly any position to marry."

"You are an officer in the militia."

He rolled his eyes as though to remind Darcy he hardly considered it a boon. "I must make to you an unfortunate confession. I have been obliged to leave the regiment on account of some debts of honor which were very pressing indeed."

"The position I acquired for you." Why would Wickham regard that any more highly than any other Darcy beneficence he had enjoyed?

"Without my consent, I might remind you. Surely, you did not expect me to eschew all recreation whilst suffering your fate for me. I hardly see what your bother is with it. I am simply doing as I must."

"Despite the fact the young lady," yes, it was hard to apply that description to her, but still, to honor Miss Elizabeth's sister, he would try, "will suffer for it."

"She has made her own choices, and the consequences of them belong solely to her." Wickham blinked—no doubt trying to affect an innocence which he certainly did not possess. He knew exactly who would be damaged and by how much.

Blackguard.

"What of your own future? Where will you go? How will you live?" Darcy tapped his fingertips together, waiting. Father had done the same thing.

"I have given that no little thought, but I have no great answer for you. I will get by somehow, I always have." How could he manage such an air of pathos in the midst of such guilt?

"Why do you not marry Lydia at once? Though her father is not very rich, I imagine he would be able to do something for you. Your situation will be largely benefited."

"I suppose you are correct. Some good might come out of it. But hardly enough, I think." Wickham sneered. "I am not ready to throw myself away upon a young woman of such a meager fortune. I shall marry, do not doubt that, but I need a woman of greater means. I think from the continent, perhaps. Yes, I shall go there."

It was tempting to ask how, precisely, he thought to get to the continent, but that was a moot point. Wickham had not thought of that until just this moment. It was simply his opening salvo in a familiar game.

Darcy stifled a sigh of relief. Now he had Wickham committed to a negotiation. Granted, it might take some time, but Darcy would win; he would give Wickham no alternative, for this was not about Lydia's hand, but the opportunity to pursue Miss

Elizabeth's, a prize worth no less than Darcy's own life and breath.

~❧~

Less than a week after his arrival in London, Darcy's efforts bore their perfect fruit. He finally found Wickham's price which, while dear, was nothing to the value of Miss Elizabeth. If Wickham only knew the truth, he would probably do himself an injury knowing how much more Darcy would have offered to have the matter settled.

But Darcy would keep that detail to himself, especially as it was only the first step. He had been high-handed in determining that Lydia and Wickham should marry and in naming a price for the bride. In truth, he had no right to do so. Thus, now he had to apply to her relations for the privilege of being their benefactor. Miss Elizabeth would approve of nothing less than his humility.

And she had to approve.

Only a little effort revealed that both Mr. Bennet and Mr. Gardiner were in town seeking the recalcitrant girl. Mr. Bennet was perhaps the most proper person to apply to, but he would have no reason to understand why Darcy even knew of the family's hardship in the first place. That could make him difficult to persuade. Some men had the alarming habit of being stubborn when it suited their best interests not to be. Surely, Mr. Bennet would be one of those. At least, Mr. Gardiner would understand Darcy's interest in the matter, so that would be the better place to begin.

A plump, neat housekeeper welcomed him into the first-rate townhouse on Gracechurch Street and led him back to Mr. Gardiner's study. The house was well appointed, and by his first impression of the housekeeper, well run. The mistress, he was told, had only just returned from a sojourn in the country to visit her sister in Hertfordshire.

She had seen Miss Elizabeth so recently! Perhaps later, he might speak with Mrs. Gardiner and glean some inkling of how Miss Elizabeth fared. But not until all the business was done.

Gardiner's study reminded him of his own: bright, neat, and well-ordered. Yellow walls reflected the sunlight onto a full bookcase behind a desk bearing tidy stacks of papers and journals. Work—real, honest work—was accomplished in this place.

"Mr. Darcy, how good it is to see you." Mr. Gardiner rose from his seat behind his desk and walked around it to meet Darcy. "To what may I owe this visit? I am surprised you are not still at Pemberley." He gestured toward a pair of wingchairs near the fireplace for them to sit.

"I think my reason for being here rather than Derbyshire is quite similar to your own. It is what has brought me here."

"I do not have the privilege of understanding you." Mr. Gardiner leaned forward, elbows pressing onto his knees.

"Forgive me if I am direct. I have found Mr. Wickham." Darcy sat back.

Mr. Gardiner's jaw dropped. "Mr. Wickham? But why would you seek him out?"

Darcy raked a hand through his hair. "I learned of your family's hardship from Miss Elizabeth herself. The letters informing her of the situation came to Pemberley as she and I were conversing. At the first news, I determined I must do everything in my power to make things right."

"How is it that you take such interest in these matters?" Mr. Gardiner's eyes narrowed just a bit. His suspicion stung Darcy's pride, but considering the circumstances, it really was not untoward.

"As I see it, the whole is the result of my mistaken pride. I have heretofore thought it beneath me to lay my private actions open to the world. I believed my character should speak for itself. Therefore, it is my duty to step forward and endeavor to remedy an evil which had been brought on by myself."

Mr. Gardiner grumbled and folded his arms over his chest. "I do not see how my niece's impetuous actions are owed to any behavior of yours. It was not you who interfered with her or even drew Wickham's attention toward her."

"But I was in a place to have prevented everything. I am convinced that had Wickham's worthlessness been well-known, it would have made it impossible for any young woman of character to love or confide in him. At the very least, her family and friends would have known to protect her from his machinations."

"How would you know of Mr. Wickham's character?"

"I have shared the entire matter in the confidence of Miss Elizabeth. Is that not enough?" Darcy closed his eyes and gritted his teeth.

"Not in this case."

Damn it all, the man was right. Darcy owed him the full truth, so he briefly recounted the details of the events at Ramsgate. "So, you can see that not only would I have known of his character, but I also had information to use in finding him to which you were not privy and which only added weight to my initial impulses."

Mr. Gardiner looked over Darcy's shoulder, nodding, considering. "Your motives do not disgrace you, sir. What have you discovered?"

"I have spoken with Wickham at length and had an audience with your niece as well. Although I offered her a means of escape, she would have nothing of it, insisting that she and Wickham would be wed."

"By the way you say that I suspect—"

"You are right to be suspicious, for after interrogating him, I am quite certain he had no intention of being married to her."

Mr. Gardiner's shoulder's sagged. "Then hope is lost, there is no remedy—"

"I said he had no intention, not that he has no intention now."

"You will have to explain."

"He is seeking advantage and hopes to gain it through marriage. I simply offered a means by which he might gain that advantage though marriage to Miss Lydia."

"I need you to be far more specific." Mr. Gardiner steepled his hands before his chest.

"There is no need. I have settled the matter to his satisfaction. You have no need to be concerned. No, that is not true; there is a part of this I must entrust to you. I do not wish to be assigned credit for this resolution. It is enough that I know it has been done. In fact, I insist."

Gardiner propped his elbows on the chair and sat up very straight. "You suggest that instead of being of use to my niece, I instead merely put up with the credit for having done so? No, I cannot. I absolutely cannot."

"I will accept nothing less."

It was to the credit of the man that he argued so vociferously to be of use to his family, but in the end, he capitulated. Reluctantly.

"I insist, though, upon knowing for which actions and decisions I will have to accept credit."

Darcy blushed. "His debts are to be paid, amounting, I believe, to more than a thousand pounds. Another thousand in addition to her own will be settled upon her, and his commission in the regulars purchased as he must have some useful occupation."

"You have done too much." Mr. Gardiner pressed his lips in a thoughtful frown.

"I have done what is necessary and nothing less."

"But her father must bear a share of the blame in this affair and should feel some burden upon himself for it. It is only right and fair and proper. The settlements must say that he should provide the couple one hundred pounds per annum in addition to what you have done."

"That was not part of the agreement. You know whatever Wickham is given will be squandered in one way or another."

"I understand that, but it just might make Bennet feel his error a bit more and encourage him to be more responsible towards his other daughters."

Darcy huffed. "I doubt it." But, if it were something that could be of help to Miss Elizabeth, how could he possible object? "I will concede the point, though. You will write to him then and tell him the matter is settled? And you will have the girl married from here, at the earliest possible date?"

"You can be assured of our support with Lydia. But, and I hate to speculate so, are you certain that Mr. Wickham will not think twice of slipping into the parson's noose?"

"I will act as his witness and ensure he is at the church at the appointed time."

"I have no doubt that will be sufficient. I will write to my brother of the happy news immediately."

Chapter 6

THE WEDDING TOOK place on the last day of August. Wickham made some small attempts to talk his way out of the matter, but in the end, he thought better of it. Surely, even he could realize the likelihood of having a better settlement on the continent was highly unlikely. Especially if Darcy began to write to his connections there and tell them of Wickham's schemes. Darcy had intimated—subtly and gently, of course—that it was a possibility if Wickham fled.

After the marriage lines were signed, Darcy watched them walk out of the church and sighed. The tension that had held him together for the past weeks ebbed away. The sensation left him almost giddy. Miss Elizabeth and her family were out of danger now.

His muse rewarded him with several nights of peaceful sleep on the journey back to Pemberley.

Perhaps she understood that he fully intended to persuade Bingley to return to Netherfield and resume his acquaintance with Miss Bennet. He could not, in good conscience, insist Bingley marry her; that would be too much. But if the affections and wishes of both were steady and unchanged, all they needed was proximity, and it would be accomplished.

Apparently, his muse was willing to recognize the attempt, allowing him to produce several tolerable sketches in his book at the inns they stayed at on their way back to Hertfordshire. Should his soul sing at such thin affirmation? Probably not, but it did anyway.

They arrived in Hertfordshire near sunset on a day bearing an uncanny similarity to the day he and Bingley had first arrived these many months ago. Darcy's hands itched; his feet longed to make haste to Longbourn and lay before her all he had done.

The knot in his stomach warned that impatience would be a mistake. To try to sway her with such offerings would somehow diminish the purity of her acceptance. No, he would muster every iota of self-control and—finally—do it all right.

And pray his restraint did not cost him as dearly as his impulsiveness had.

His muse was nothing if not fickle.

Mundane business at Netherfield occasioned by Bingley's prolonged absence took up the following two days. Thankfully, Darcy was there to help, or it would surely have taken a week to complete.

On the third day, Bingley insisted their horses be readied for a call upon Longbourn. Granted, he had rather a great deal of subtle help in deciding upon that action, but ultimately it was his decision.

The way Bingley paced and muttered while waiting for the horses might have been laughable had it not carried such an important message. His anxiety at the sort of reception Miss Bennet might offer him was a sure sign that his affections towards her were of the real sort, unchanged by their separation. Excellent.

The Longbourn housekeeper showed Bingley and him into the parlor. Mrs. Bennet's shrill whispers—instructions to her daughters on how to present themselves—passed through the walls as effectively as if she were in the hall shouting. Truly, most mothers would do the same sort of thing, but in a more civilized tone of voice so as not to be overheard. Could he fault Mrs. Bennet for poor vocal control? Yes, he could, but today he would not. If the housekeeper and Bingley could pretend to ignore them, then so would he.

The parlor was unchanged from the way he remembered it: furniture a touch shabby and faded from too much sun, no painting of any note on the walls, haphazardly placed items that most would call decorative but he thought cluttered. Yet, it was a warm and happy place, so much the more so for the presence of the one person he most longed for.

Miss Bennet and Miss Elizabeth sat together on a couch near the window, their color high. The sunlight brought out a luster in Miss Elizabeth's fine eyes that must be a sign--surely, it must. He held his breath and steeled himself. He had come too far to give into temptation now.

They rose and curtsied.

"Good day, Mr. Bingley, Mr. Darcy." Miss Bennet's gentle, warm voice betrayed no trace of bitterness or resentment. The flush on her cheeks and forehead betrayed her agitation, but with no hint of reproach, it portended well indeed.

"We are most delighted to see you have returned to the neighborhood. The society here truly suffered from your absence. Pray sit down." Mrs. Bennet gestured toward a pair of chairs, which were much too far away from Miss Elizabeth but would have to do for the moment. "You are most kind to call upon us. I am sure you must have a great many things to do and a great many amusements open to you. That you should think of us …."

And so, the banal chatter began. It might bother him more if Bingley were not here to keep up the other side of the conversation. But he was, so Darcy could content himself to observe the entire scene, especially Miss Elizabeth. No commentary he might offer could improve upon that privilege. He was in her presence, and she was content if a bit surprised. Her shock offered its own delights: the most intriguing dimple appeared on her cheek when she was surprised.

Still, he really ought to attempt to say something. It was only polite, and he dare not be uncivil. "How are your Aunt and Uncle Gardiner? Are they in good health?"

Miss Elizabeth uttered a small gasp and stammered something like a reply. She shifted her feet and clutched her hands, limbs stiff, as though trying not to spring to her feet.

She knew something. Merciful heavens! What did she know and how?

He had sworn the Gardiners to secrecy. They were honorable people and would not betray him. Who could have …?

Oh! That twitterpated girl! No doubt she forgot her promise of silence in the excitement of showing off her new husband to her sisters. She probably felt the need to brag about her wedding and who was in attendance.

Stupid, stupid girl! Had she ruined everything?

Miss Elizabeth settled a bit and gazed into his eyes, asking, seeking, wondering. He willed himself not to look away, to open to her anything she wanted to see. Oh, the exquisite torture of having his reserve stripped away layer by layer by those eyes!

"It is a long time, Mr. Bingley, since you went away." Had anyone ever told Mrs. Bennet she sounded far too much like a squawking goose?

"Yes, it has been. Far too long I think, to be away from such pleasant surrounds and pleasant people." Bingley nodded vigorously, his eyes not leaving Miss Bennet.

"I began to be afraid you would never come back again. People did say you meant to quit the place entirely at Michaelmas. I hope it is not true. A great many changes have happened in the neighborhood since you went away. Miss Lucas is married and settled." Did the woman ever stop to breathe? "And one of my own daughters. I suppose you have heard of it; indeed, you must have seen it in the papers. It was in the *Times* and the *Courier*, I know; though it was not put in as it ought to be. It was only said, 'Lately, George Wickham, Esq. to Miss Lydia Bennet,' without there being a syllable said of her father, or the place where she lived, or anything. It was my brother Gardiner's drawing up too, and I wonder how he came to make such an awkward business of it. Did you see it?"

Actually, it had been Darcy's suggestion to leave the Bennet's name and location off the announcement to spare the Miss Bennets unnecessary embarrassment.

"I did indeed. My most hearty congratulations to the couple and to yourselves. I hope that it will be a very happy match for all concerned." Bingley's voice turned just a little flat, but Mrs. Bennet did not appear to recognize the change.

Miss Elizabeth did, though, abruptly looking away, a flush rising up from her shoulders. For whom did she blush? Her mother or her sister?

"It is a delightful thing, to be sure, to have a daughter well married." Mrs. Bennet smoothed her skirt over her lap. "But at the same time, Mr. Bingley, it is very hard to have her taken such a way from me. They are gone down to Newcastle, a place quite northward, it seems, and there they are to stay I do not know how long. His regiment is there, for I suppose you have heard of his leaving the Derbyshire, and of his being gone into the regulars. Thank Heaven! He has some friends, though perhaps not so many as he deserves." Mrs. Bennet cast a quick dark glace at Darcy.

The daughter knew what the mother did not. What a mercy! Mrs. Bennet's gratitude would be far worse than her scorn.

Miss Elizabeth all but writhed in her seat, every posture attesting to the shame she suffered. Did that mean she approved of his interference?

"Do you—and your guest—mean to make any stay in the country at present? It would be a shame to lose your company quickly." Honeyed warmth returned to Mrs. Bennet's voice.

"A few weeks, I believe. Perhaps more, if we find it pleasing." Bingley glanced at him, brows raised.

"You are here for the hunting then? Of course, you are. You young men are all about sport. You must know, when you have killed all your own birds, Mr. Bingley, I beg you will come here, and shoot as many as you please on Mr. Bennet's manor. I am sure he will be vastly happy to oblige you and will save all the best of the coveys for you."

Miss Elizabeth clutched her temples and not without good reason. Was it wrong to be delighted at her discomfort? Not that he would have her discomfited for his own pleasure, but for what it all meant—at least what it might mean, what it should mean.

Thankfully, Bingley was somehow able to wrest the conversation back from Mrs. Bennet—how he managed was a feat that should be studied and taken down for posterity, so momentous was it. He began talking about his tour that led to Derbyshire and Pemberley, wisely leaving out the time he had spent in London as he regaled them with beauty of the landscapes and the most interesting people they had met along the way.

Miss Bennet seemed rapt by his conversations, rising to a new beauty in his presence, almost fairy-like in its quality. He had never seen her like this. How could he have missed it? Is this what Bingley saw when he gazed upon her?

And to think Darcy had the audacity to interfere? No wonder his muse had been offended!

Had he done enough to atone for his errors?

Somewhere in the house a longcase clock chimed. "Pray forgive us. I am certain we have overstayed our welcome. We must be going." Bingley rose, but slowly. None who saw him could doubt his very material reluctance to depart.

Mrs. Bennet stood. "You are quite a visit in my debt, Mr. Bingley, for when you went to town last winter, you promised to take a family dinner with us as soon as you returned. I have not forgotten, you see; and I assure you, I was very much disappointed that you did not come back and keep your engagement."

Bingley shrugged. "I do regret having been prevented by business—"

"Then you would consider having dinner with us on Tuesday. Both of you, of course."

Bingley glanced at him, and Darcy nodded.

"Certainly. We will be there and look forward to your gracious hospitality."

Though he cared nothing for Mrs. Bennet's hospitality, it meant his muse was smiling. He would see Miss Elizabeth once again on Tuesday. What better sign could he hope for?

<hr>

On Tuesday, there was a large party assembled at Longbourn when Darcy and Bingley arrived. Darcy checked his first instinct to tell Bingley to offer his regrets and return back to Netherfield. How dare Mrs. Bennet surprise him with a large dinner party! Such things were difficult enough when he had opportunity to properly prepare, but this? It was beyond the pale.

But to flee Longbourn's hospitality would require an untruth to be told. He abhorred disguise even more than surprise company. And so did his muse.

He dragged himself inside.

When they repaired to the dining-room, it seemed Miss Elizabeth eagerly watched to see whether Bingley would take the place, which, in all their former parties had belonged to him, by Miss Bennet. Her prudent mother forbore to invite Bingley to sit by herself—an impressive feat for certain, but a prudent one, given what she was likely hoping to accomplish. Would it amuse her—or Miss Elizabeth—to know that he harbored the same hopes for his friend as they?

On entering the room, Bingley seemed to hesitate, but Miss Bennet happened to look round, and happened to smile. He placed himself by her.

Elizabeth glanced at Darcy as he smiled and nodded at Bingley. How her face lit, a great fire warming his soul. Approbation! He had her approbation! What more could he possibly want in the world? Did it matter that he sat beside Mrs. Bennet at dinner? Did it matter that Sir William Lucas prattled on endlessly on his other side? No. Not even that could overshadow her smiles.

Hopefully, the evening would yet afford some opportunity of bringing Miss Elizabeth together with him. Surely, the whole of the visit could not pass away without enabling them to enter into something more than the mere ceremony of greetings that attended his entrance.

Perhaps after dinner.

The gentlemen went into the drawing room following dinner, but with Miss Bennet making tea and Miss Elizabeth pouring coffee in so close a confederacy around the table, there was not a single vacancy near her which would admit a chair. Perhaps he might get closer to her if he sought out a cup of coffee.

"Is your sister at Pemberley still?" Something like desperation tinged her voice, but it did not match her words. Was she anxious to have some conversation with him?

"Yes, she will remain there till Christmas."

"And quite alone? Have all her friends left her?" Miss Elizabeth poured a cup of coffee, her hands trembling with the effort.

"Mrs. Annesley is with her. The others have been gone on to Scarborough these three weeks."

She looked as though she wanted to say more but was interrupted by one of the local young ladies. Darcy walked away. Yes, he was disappointed, but what could he expect in such a crowded affair?

The material point was that she had spoken to him, asked after the family dearest to him. If that was not auspicious, what was? Yes, this had been a very good evening, indeed.

Upon leaving Longbourn that night, his course was clear—a bit of a nuisance, but clear. But with so much favor having been doled out to him, he could not, he did not deviate from his path for mere inconvenience. He had so taxed the grace of his muse that there would surely be no more second chances.

The next morning, he found Bingley in the morning room, sipping his coffee and reading the paper. Though the room had not changed from his last sojourn there, it was different. Was it Bingley's current disposition that made the sun a little brighter and the breakfast offerings more fragrant? The aroma of nutmeg was particularly pronounced.

"You seem rather well-pleased this morning."

Darcy sat down across the round, walnut table from him.

"In fact, I am." Bingley folded his paper and set it aside. "Though I am concerned you will not approve."

"Why would you think that?" Darcy's fingers closed around his coffee cup.

"It is on a matter over which I understood you had some rather strong opinions."

"I see." Oh, to be able to nudge Bingley along and make him come out with it already! "Is it something you wish to discuss?"

"No, actually I do not wish to discuss it at all." Bingley squared his shoulders. "I am not actually certain I care about your opinion at all."

Truly? Had he just said that? Excellent! "I am intrigued as to the matter under consideration."

"No, you are just being difficult. You well know it." Bingley scowled--he actually scowled!

"You have said nothing, so how can I know?"

"It is Miss Bennet. I know you do not approve; you think her family is below me and will be a detriment to me." Bingley pressed his hands to the table. "But I do not care."

"Excellent!"

Bingley jerked back and blinked thrice. "What did you say?"

He must not laugh. Definitely, he must not laugh. "I said that is excellent. While I thought to do you a service, I was in fact wrong to interfere and try to decide upon the means by which you might be happy."

Bingley cocked his head, still blinking. "Did I just hear you correctly? Did you just admit that you were in error?"

"Completely and without reservation."

The look of astonishment on Bingley's face was priceless. It would have to make it into his sketchbook soon.

"So, if I were to go there now, for a private interview with her—"

"I would applaud your good sense."

"Truly? You are not jesting?"

"Have I ever jested about such a thing?" Had he ever jested about anything at all?

Bingley threw his napkin on the table and stood. "I have a call to make."

"Do what you need to. I must go to town to manage some business. But count on it, I shall return in ten days and fully expect to offer my congratulations when I arrive." Darcy stood.

He had not exactly told Bingley to make an offer of marriage. That would be interfering, and he would not do that again. But suggesting his approval of such an action, that was surely acceptable.

Bingley nodded and grinned—a silly, boyish expression that he tended toward when words escaped him. Another expression that demanded a sketch.

His muse approved. But the sketch would have to wait.

⸺⟡⸺

Not long after Bingley's departure, Darcy left for London. With Bingley's pursuit of Miss Bennet underway, there was only one thing left for him to do. A call to his solicitor was in order. He would not approach Miss Elizabeth without settlement papers—generous ones—already in hand. If that did not persuade her that he was utterly serious when he renewed his offer, nothing would.

And if they did not, would his soul survive?

Agony squeezed through his chest. No, if he dwelt upon that possibility, darkness would close over him, and he might never rise again. He pulled out his sketchbook and struggled to capture Bingley's astonished expression. That promise of joy and hope was what he needed now.

Darcy paced the floor as he waited for the solicitor to draw up the necessary papers. Even knowing that it would take time did nothing to ease the tension that opened a gaping maw before him and threatened to swallow him whole. He had tried to write letters, conduct other business, but the efforts were futile. The only things left to him were adding sketches to his book—all his muse permitted him were images of her sister, her mother, Bingley, even Sir William, but not Miss Elizabeth—and pacing. The carpet was beginning to show a distinct pattern of wear.

The doorbell rang.

No one but his solicitor knew he was in town. Who could possibly be calling?

The housekeeper announced Aunt Catherine and brought her to his study. Heavens above!

"Aunt Catherine?" He stood and glanced about. The room was tidy and should be above reproach. How did she manage to elicit such a reaction from him in his own home?

She stood before him wrapped in layers of fine fabric and indignation. "I am very pleased to find you here before you made a very foolish mistake. Sit down and listen well to what I have to say."

He sat and bit his tongue. There was little point in trying to interrupt her.

She settled upon a plump chair and smoothed her skirts over her lap. "I have waited long enough. I insist you make your engagement to Anne official."

"Excuse me?"

"You heard me clear enough. You must act now. You are in danger, and I will see you protected." She rapped her knuckles on the edge of his desk.

"Exactly what sort of danger am I in?"

"From strumpets and fortune hunters."

"I see no such persons here." He cast about his study for good measure.

She threw both hands in the air. "Men can be such fools! I am certain with her arts and allurements, she has turned your eyes away from her true nature."

"Of whom do you speak?"

"Of Miss Elizabeth Bennet."

His heart thundered, and he missed her next several speeches.

"She is without morals, without regard for your good name and the good name of her family. She is motivated by advantage, trying to step outside the sphere to which she was born. It is not to be tolerated. She must be taught a lesson. When you announce your engagement to Anne—"

"How precisely would you know this about her? You have not seen her since she was in Kent, and I am quite certain she was not at all of such a mind then." He clutched his forehead.

"Of course, she was not. In my presence at Rosings, she was aware of her place. But she has had time to think, to plan, to scheme just how to catch you unawares. I will not have it." She waved her hands as though that settled the matter.

"You have not answered my question. How come you by this knowledge?"

"I paid a call to her just yesterday."

The blood drained from his face. "You went all the way to Hertfordshire, driving for so many days to pay a call on her?"

"Of course, I did! News of such an alarming nature had reached me that there was nothing else to be done."

"What sort of news?"

"I was told that not only was Miss Bennet on the point of being most advantageously married, but that Miss Elizabeth Bennet, would, in all likelihood, be soon afterwards united to my nephew, my own nephew. That is you! Can you imagine? Though I know it must be a scandalous falsehood, though I would not injure you so much as to suppose the truth of it possible, I instantly resolved on setting off to confront this girl and make my sentiments known."

"And what did she say?" He could hardly force the words out.

Aunt Catherine's eyes bulged like an over-excited pug. "She told me I was not entitled to know her dearest concerns and nothing could induce her to be explicit. She did not care that you were engaged to my daughter."

"But I am not!"

"Nor would she satisfy me with a promise to never become engaged with you."

His knees melted until he finally sat on the edge of his desk. "She said that?"

"Indeed, she did! The cheek, the audacity! I am not accustomed to being spoken to in that manner. I warned her that a woman like her, married to you, should not expect to be noticed by your family or friends. She would be censured, slighted, and despised by everyone connected to you. The alliance would be a disgrace, and her name never mentioned."

"And her response?" He forced back an anticipatory smile.

Aunt Catherine tossed her head, her lip curling back. "She said, 'These are heavy misfortunes indeed, but the wife of Mr. Darcy must have such extraordinary sources of happiness necessarily attached to her situation, that she could upon the whole have no cause to repine.'"

Aunt Catherine continued on in that vein for some time, but none of her words drowned out that one chorus that played over and over in his mind: *extraordinary sources of happiness.*

The moment Aunt Catherine stormed from Darcy House, he dashed upstairs to his attic studio and painted long into the night.

<hr>

The next day, the solicitor finished his task, and Darcy was off to Hertfordshire that very evening, arriving at Netherfield after dinner when dusk was about to give way to dark. To say Bingley was surprised might have been an overstatement. It seemed he was aware of very little except his own good fortune which he could not help but impart to Darcy.

Bingley was now betrothed to Miss Bennet. Her father had readily given his blessing to the match. Mrs. Bennet was sharing their happiness with any who would listen—and probably a few who did not. Miss Bennet had forgiven Bingley his inconstancy and proved it with her angelic tranquility. Was there any woman more perfect? Moreover, Bingley did not blame Darcy for his part in the matter, and expected to be duly thanked for his graciousness in that choice.

Whilst Darcy offered his congratulations to Bingley, if he were to be entirely honest, he congratulated himself on overcoming the penultimate hurdle to his own happiness without raising the censure of his muse. Perhaps this boded well for him and his mission for the morrow.

It would have been pleasant to coax Bingley to say more of his mode of declaration and how exactly he won Miss Bennet's agreement. But what pleased Miss Bennet would find less approval from Miss Elizabeth.

For this he was truly on his own. Except for his muse. Surely, she would support him.

They arrived very early at Longbourn, but Bingley's presence there was universally welcome, so the hour made little difference to the residents. Bingley proposed walking out—no doubt in hopes of being alone with Miss Bennet on the road. Sadly, Miss Kitty chose to join them and walked with him and Miss Elizabeth.

Not just with them but between them.

To be so close and unable to say anything of substance! Surely this must be some final test? What else could explain this turn of luck? Patient, he would be patient. He had not come so far to lose it all now. So, he listened to talk of ribbon and muslin and sleeves.

Torture, simply torture.

By Miss Bennet's preferences, they walked towards the Lucases', and Miss Kitty was seized by a desire to call upon Miss Lucas, leaving him to walk more or less alone with Miss Elizabeth.

Now, he could speak now! But first, he must draw a breath.

"Mr. Darcy, I am a very selfish creature, and, for the sake of giving relief to my own feelings, care not how much I may be wounding yours. I can no longer help thanking you for your unexampled kindness to my poor sister. Ever since I have known it, I have been most anxious to acknowledge to you how gratefully I feel it. Were it known to the rest of my family, I should not have merely my own gratitude to express."

Darcy clasped his hands behind his back and bowed his head. His steps crunched on the road gravel, little clouds of dust swirling around each footfall. "I am sorry, exceedingly sorry, that you have ever been informed of what may, in a mistaken light, have given you uneasiness. How did you come to know?"

"You must not blame my aunt. Lydia's thoughtlessness first betrayed to me that you had been concerned in the matter, and, of course, I could not rest till I knew the particulars. Let me thank you again and again, in the name of all my family, for that generous compassion which induced you to take so much trouble and bear so many mortifications, for the sake of discovering them." From the corner of his eye, he could make out the endearing way she chewed her lower lip.

"If you will thank me, let it be for yourself alone. That the wish of giving happiness to you might add force to the other inducements which led me on, I shall not attempt to deny. But your family owe me nothing. Much as I respect them, I believe I thought only of you."

She did not respond! Oh, that she would say something!

He must wait for her to speak. He must. But something overwhelmed him and tore the words from him. "You are too generous to trifle with me. If your feelings are still what they were last April, tell me so at once. My affections and wishes are unchanged, but one word from you will silence me on this subject forever." Heart thundering in his ears, the world blurred before him, but he forced himself to walk on.

This moment would decide his fate. Forever.

And still she did not speak. Her cheeks flushed the deepest rose, and her eyes grew very bright, shimmering like moonlight on a stream. But what that could mean?

She pressed her hands to her cheeks. "My feelings…oh, my feelings! They have so materially changed, I cannot think of what they were then without dread. Pray do not ever remind me of what I said or felt last spring. I would just as soon never consider it again."

He drew in a slow, unsteady breath, chest trembling. "Am I to understand then, that you might consider a different response to the offer I made then?"

How many heartbeats must pass before she gave him an answer. Twenty? Thirty?

"Yes."

All the air rushed form his lungs. He barely held himself upright. "Pray, forgive me and tell me again, lest I am mistaken and have misunderstood in order to hear what I would most desire."

"Yes, my response would be very different." She looked up at him, a generous smile dimpling her cheeks. "If you are renewing your offer, then I would tell you yes."

"Not from gratitude for the service to your sister, pray assure me of that."

"What if it were? Would it not be natural?" She lifted an eyebrow, eyes twinkling. Was she teasing?

"Natural, yes, but insufficient. I could not have you attached to me because of mere gratitude alone. At one time it would have been enough. But truly, I want more."

"What do you want, Mr. Darcy?"

"I want your heart, your soul, connected to mine. Intertwined, a part of one another for every day forward. It is a very great deal to ask, I know, and I am loath to say it aloud for fear it is too much." How had those words, almost too intimate to speak, been wrenched from his lips?

"It is a great deal. But it is not too much." She walked on. "I have come to understand you are hardly who I thought you were. Quite the opposite in fact— I am ashamed to have been so mistaken in my own pride. I have never met another to whom I feel so utterly connected, so utterly at home with, whom I long to be with again and again."

"And you will not regret quitting Hertfordshire and all you know here?"

"To pollute the shades of Pemberley?"

He stopped and stared at her. "Heavens above, pray tell me that my aunt did not say such a thing to you."

"I will not lie to you." She pressed her lips as though determined to keep a secret.

"I am mortified beyond what I can express." He dragged his hand down his face. She was not the only one with embarrassing relatives.

His muse kicked him. How long had she been working to get him to see just that?

Miss Elizabeth offered a tiny lift of her shoulders, matched by a tilt of her head. How gracious she was not to rail at the incivility of Aunt Catherine.

"In an odd way, I have her to thank for this moment. She came to me in London to report the conversation she had with you. It taught me to hope as I had scarcely ever allowed myself to hope before. I knew enough of your disposition to be certain that, had you been absolutely, irrevocably decided against me, you would have acknowledged it to Lady Catherine, frankly and openly."

Elizabeth laughed and shielded the side of her face nearest him with her hand. "Yes, you know enough of my frankness to believe me capable of that. After abusing you so abominably to your face, I could have no scruple in abusing you to all your relations."

"What did you say of me that I did not deserve? My behavior to you at the time had merited the severest reproof. It was unpardonable. I cannot think of it without abhorrence. Your reproof, so well applied, I shall never forget: 'had you behaved in a more gentleman-like manner.' Those were your words. You know not, you can scarcely conceive, how they have tortured me. You thought me devoid of every proper feeling. The turn of your countenance I shall never forget as you said that I could not have addressed you in any possible way that would induce you to accept me." Now was probably not the time to tell her he had since captured it in his sketchbook and might just paint it.

"Oh! do not repeat what I then said. These recollections will not do at all. I assure you that I have long been most heartily ashamed of it." She ducked her head demurely.

"Did my letter soon make you think better of me? Did you, on reading it, give any credit to its contents?"

She lifted her head, nodding. "Indeed, I did. I have read it so many times, and with each reading all my former prejudices were removed."

"I hope you have destroyed the letter. There was one part especially, the opening of it, which I should dread your having the power of reading again. I can remember some expressions which might justly make you hate me."

"The letter shall certainly be burnt if you believe it essential to the preservation of my regard." She offered him a sidelong glance, dimples evident. "But you must learn some of my philosophy. Think only of the past as its remembrance gives you pleasure."

"But with me, it is not so. Painful recollections will intrude which cannot, which ought not, to be repelled. I have been a selfish being all my life in practice, though not in principle. As a child I was taught what was right, but I was not taught to correct my temper. I was given good principles but was left to follow them in pride and conceit—allowed, encouraged, almost taught to be selfish and overbearing; to care for none beyond my own family circle; to think meanly of all the rest of the world. Such a man I might still have been but for you, dearest, loveliest Elizabeth!"

Those words brought a blush and a glimmer to her eyes. Better still, now he could utter those sentiments freely, as often as he liked.

"What do I not owe you! By you, I was properly humbled. My object since then has been to show you by every civility in my power. I hoped to obtain your forgiveness, to lessen your ill opinion, by letting you see that your reproofs had been attended to. And that my wishes had never changed."

Her brow creased just a bit. "But some opinions have changed. I must ask whether you were surprised to learn of Jane and Mr. Bingley?"

"Not at all. When I went away to London, I felt that it would soon happen."

"That is to say, you had given your permission? I guessed as much." And everything in her countenance said she approved.

"Before my going to London, I made a confession to him. I told him that I believed myself mistaken in supposing that your sister was indifferent to him, and as I could easily perceive that his attachment to her was unabated, I felt no doubt of their happiness together. He was angry, just a bit, as he is not one prone to such emotions. But his anger, I am persuaded, lasted no longer than he remained in any doubt of your sister's sentiments. He has heartily forgiven me now."

"I can see how forgiveness would be in his nature."

"And what of yours? Honestly, can you tell me you have forgiven me?" Was he tempting his fate by asking?

"Totally and completely. I dearly hope you feel the same towards me."

They stopped and stood toe to toe. What words could possibly express what swelled his heart? He took her shoulders in his hands and leaned down.

Their lips met, and his tension melted away,

threatening to reduce him to his knees there in the middle of the road.

"Can you detect any sign of resentment in me?" he whispered near her ear.

"Indeed not. Only what you once promised me: your ardent affection."

"Ever and always."

❧ Epilogue

HAPPY FOR ALL her maternal feelings was the day on which Mrs. Bennet got rid of her two most deserving daughters, and Darcy's muse finally rested in the satisfaction of his being united with the one who was most perfectly suited to being his helpmeet, his inspiration, and occasionally his guide. Standing with her before the vicar, wholeness settled over him; contentment filled his being. Not long after, they were away to London where his life might finally and truly begin.

That night, his muse awaited him upstairs in a chamber carefully prepared. Silver moonlight bathed her porcelain form, completing the transformation from earthly to ethereal. He surrendered to her intimate embrace. Surrounded by a completeness he could never have imagined, his soul shattered into a cascade of colors he could hear, a thousand sensations he could see. But somehow, they all made sense in communion with the other half of his soul.

Acknowledgments

So many people have helped me along the journey taking this from an idea to a reality.

Debbie, Susanne, Julie, Anji, and Ruth thank you so much for cold reading, proofing and being honest!

And my dear friend Cathy, my biggest cheerleader, you have kept me from chickening out more than once!

And my sweet sister Gerri who believed in even those first attempts that now live in the file drawer!

Thank you!

Other Books by Maria Grace

Remember the Past
The Darcy Brothers

A Jane Austen Regency Life Series:
A Jane Austen Christmas: Regency Christmas Traditions
Courtship and Marriage in Jane Austen's World
How Jane Austen Kept her Cook: An A to Z History of Georgian Ice Cream

Jane Austen's Dragons Series:
A Proper Introduction to Dragons
Pemberley: Mr. Darcy's Dragon
Longbourn: Dragon Entail
Netherfield: Rogue Dragon

The Queen of Rosings Park Series:
Mistaking Her Character
The Trouble to Check Her
A Less Agreeable Man

Sweet Tea Stories:
A Spot of Sweet Tea: Hopes and Beginnings (short story anthology)
Snowbound at Hartfield
A Most Affectionate Mother
Inspiration

Darcy Family Christmas Series:
Darcy and Elizabeth: Christmas 1811
The Darcy's First Christmas
From Admiration to Love

Given Good Principles Series:
Darcy's Decision
The Future Mrs. Darcy
All the Appearance of Goodness
Twelfth Night at Longbourn

Behind the Scenes Anthologies (with Austen Variations):
Pride and Prejudice: Behind the Scenes
Persuasion: Behind the Scenes

Available in e-book and paperback

Available in paperback, e-book, and audiobook format at all online bookstores.

On Line Exclusives:

Bonus and deleted scenes
Regency Life Series

Find them at:
   www.http//RandomBitsofFascination.com

Free e-books:
Rising Waters: Hurricane Harvey Memoirs
Lady Catherine's Cat
A Gift from Rosings Park
Bits of Bobbin Lace
Half Agony, Half Hope: New Reflections on Persuasion
Four Days in April

By Austen Variations:

A Very Austen Advent
Scenes Jane Austen Never Wrote: First Anniversaries
March Madness Mashups
Anniversary February
Jane Bennet in January

✢About the Author

Maria Grace has her PhD in Educational Psychology and is a 16-year veteran of the university classroom where she taught courses in human growth and development, learning, test development and counseling. None of which have anything to do with her undergraduate studies in economics/sociology/managerial studies/behavior sciences.

She has one husband and one grandson, earned two graduate degrees and two black belts, raised three sons, danced English Country dance for four years, is aunt to five nieces, is designing a sixth Regency costume, blogged seven years on Random Bits of Fascination, has outlines for eight novels waiting to be written, attended nine English country dance balls, and shared her life with ten cats.

Her books, fiction and nonfiction, are available at all major online booksellers.

Contact her at:

author.MariaGrace@gmail.com

Facebook:

http://facebook.com/AuthorMariaGrace

On Amazon.com:

http://amazon.com/author/mariagrace

Random Bits of Fascination
(http://RandomBitsofFascination.com)

Austen Variations (http://AustenVariations.com)

English Historical Fiction Authors
(http://EnglshHistoryAuthors.blogspot.com)

White Soup Press (http://whitesouppress.com/)

On Twitter @WriteMariaGrace

On Pinterest: http://pinterest.com/mariagrace423/

Printed in Great Britain
by Amazon